I0520119

LUNA STATION
QUARTERLY

Issue 034 | June 2018

Editor-in-Chief
Jennifer Lyn Parsons

Editors
Vivian Caethe • Tawny Case • Linda Codega • Shel Graves
Cathrin Hagey • Wanda Evans • Dana Mele • Megan Patton
Danielle Perry • Imelda Wistey

LUNA STATION PRESS
NEW JERSEY

Luna Station Quarterly publishes short fiction on March 1st, June 1st,
September 1st, and December 1st. For more information and submission
guidelines, please visit our website at lunastationquarterly.com

For Luna Station Press
Creative Director - Tara Quinn Lindsey
Editor-in-Chief & Founder - Jennifer Lyn Parsons

LUNA STATION PRESS

www.lunastationpress.com

CONTENTS

Editorial

Jennifer Lyn Parsons

A software engineer by trade, Jennifer is a life-long lover of story with a capital S. Her work has been seen in various magazines and she has published three books, with quite a few more in her back pocket. She counts Jim Jarmusch and Laura Ingalls Wilder as two of her biggest influences. Make of that what you will.

When not writing either code or fiction, she reads books and comics, and sometimes makes things out of wool or paper. She finds joy in making things, be they digital or analog.

Recently I've been thinking a lot about the "Strong Female Character" trope in fiction and what strength means. Here I'm referring to the character who often has her life turned on its head and transforms from a vulnerable person into a fierce force of ass-kicking nature. Sarah Connor in the Terminator movies being a prime example.

There's nothing inherently wrong with this kind of character in the context of her story. She does what she needs to do to survive and save the world. I would hazard to argue that the only problem is the lens through which she's portrayed, which is one of violence and the stereotypical view of what strength means in our world.

However, I struggle with identifying with this kind of character as I know the strength she shows is not where my own strength lies. I am not currently a physically fit and ass-kicking person. How can I see myself and my own strengths represented while watching this kind of media? The answer is I kind of don't beyond a generalized "yay she's winning and defeating the villain", and I'm not sure what to do about that.

The crux of my struggle is that physical strength is not the only way someone can be strong. Emotional strength is just as valid and quite under appreciated and under represented in our world and in our fiction. This is where my strength is found, or at least something like it. The healers, the nurturers, the characters with strong minds and hearts, if not strong bodies.

I work in the tech industry and I see a similar dynamic played out there as well. Those of us with "soft skills" who are good at non-technical aspects of the work are further down in the respect hierarchy (and pay scale) than those with stronger technical expertise. In other words, this is not just a problem in fiction, but in our larger world.

The question is what authors can do to represent different kinds of strength while not undermining the way the world is changing for the better. It's a problem I honestly don't know how to approach. It feels that in the current climate, characters must all be self-rescuing, badass princesses because portraying them as anything else would leave a door open to back-sliding and slowing our progress.

I struggle as a writer and as an editor in telling and finding stories that don't compromise the work being done to challenge patriarchal ideas about how the world works. LSQ is built on uplift and so we work hard to keep growing and changing in ways that are supportive to the causes of feminism and equality.

But how do we do that without sacrificing a diverse view of what strength means? Are we stuck in the unfortunate position of only presenting characters that are forced into (or choose) violence as their way of remaking the world into a better place? Does that simply reinforce the idea that physical strength (or mental intelligence) is the only kind that's worth acknowledging? Where do the healers, the supporters, fit into all of this? How are they not left behind or trampled underfoot in the battle being fought on all fronts?

I am honest, dear reader, that I do not have an answer to these questions. Even in writing this editorial it was a challenge to piece out the various layers of my own conflicting feelings. I know many of you have clear thoughts on this and have found a more black and white take on the situation. I am glad for you, but for myself, the situation is more nuanced and I don't know if it will settle into clarity in my lifetime.

What I can do for now is take each story, each thought, as it comes and weigh it carefully. I can support a diversity of voices and examine my own language and thoughts. I can work hard each day to be an ally and not an enemy. Sometimes I will do better at this than others, but I will promise to always do my work with the intent of kindness and inclusivity and an open heart.

I hope you find it in yourself to do the same. Someday it will be different. It's already so much different than when I was a girl. Let's stay together and keep doing our work. The healer and the warrior need each other and there are room for both at the table.

I'll save you a seat right next to me.

L S Q | 034

You Pay Your Money and You Take Your Chance

Michelle Ann King

Michelle Ann King's stories have appeared in over seventy different venues, including Interzone, Strange Horizons, and Black Static. See www.transientcactus.co.uk for links to her published works.

This story first appeared in *Bards & Sages Quarterly*, January 2014

The smiling Time Pocket receptionist showed Disa into the waiting room. It had sofas and leather recliners, a free bar where discreet white-coated staff poured tiny measures of top class spirits, and tables laid out with finger food: miniature scones and delicate cucumber sandwiches cut into crustless triangles. It evoked a sense of separateness, of floating in a stream cut off from the rest of the world. A kind of civilised timelessness. Which was, Disa supposed, the point.

That was why they were there, after all. Timelessness. To have less time. No—to have *had* less time. A small but very important distinction.

She accepted a glass of Scotch from one of the discreet young men in white and stood at the bar. She wasn't supposed to be drinking, but then she wasn't supposed to be doing a lot of things. Not least of which was coming here. Her daughter would be furious, if she knew. But Claudie had been in a state of repressed fury ever since Disa's decision to stop treatment, so there would be nothing new there.

Claudie had been particularly enraged about this place. Unnatural, she called it. Which Disa could understand, in a way, but so were a lot of other things. Chemotherapy, for example.

And the Pocket had been discovered, hadn't it, not invented? It wasn't man-made. So didn't that make it natural by default?

Semantics, Claudie would say, with a dismissive curl of her lip. Claudie said most things dismissively, especially when she was speaking to Disa. Or about her, and her foolish, selfish choices.

Disa took a sip of her Scotch. It burned her lips, and tasted of ashes. She slid it back across the bar and the young man tipped it away without a word. Wasteful, she was. Claudie said that a lot, too.

She wastes, she is wasting, she has wasted, she will waste.

Or will she? Maybe. Maybe not. Nobody knew. That was also the point, wasn't it?

Twelve months, you got. Or lost. You went in the Pocket and you came out either a year younger, or a year older. There was no way of knowing which way it would go, but that didn't stop people from trying to work it out. There were systems aplenty, out there. Books that listed mathematical formulae based on your age, mass, height and star sign. Crystals that influenced the geothermal vibrations of the Pocket. Or, for an appropriate donation, previous clients—who were now clearly attuned to the wavelength of the timestream—would channel their energy on your behalf.

Clients like Mrs. Jaclyn Castleton, from the Isle of Wight, who'd gone through the Pocket fifteen times in a row, and went backwards every time. Fifteen years taken off, just like that. Her book, *Twenty-Five Again!* (a combination of autobiography, gambling addiction memoir and self-help guide) had recently hit number one on the *USA Today* bestseller list, even though everybody knew the title was artistic licence because her ex-husband had uploaded her birth certificate and proved she'd actually been forty-one that first time, not forty. But twenty-five was clearly a catchier number and who was going to quibble about a single year?

Well. That was the question, wasn't it?

Claudie, for instance. Claudie would quibble. Claudie would— and did—talk a lot about confirmation bias, and how Disa was only looking at the statistics that backed up what she already wanted to believe. About how there was absolutely nothing anyone could do to influence the outcome of going into the Pocket, no matter what all the books and testimonials said. That the crystals and flower essences and channelled energies were nothing but a waste of Disa's money. Which, by extension, was Claudie's money.

Foolish. Selfish.

Disa helped herself to a cucumber sandwich, but it tasted of cardboard. Slightly smoked cardboard, thanks to the memory of the Scotch. It made her feel like she'd licked out a fireplace.

She stopped chewing and looked at the bartender. He looked back at her. Would he hold out his hand and let her spit the unwanted food into it, take it back as easily and smoothly as he had the drink? Probably. It seemed like that sort of place. And he seemed like the kind of man who took last requests.

Disa swallowed her sandwich.

'I have three months to live,' she told him. 'Stage four lung cancer. If I go in the Pocket and it takes me back, I get fifteen months. A year and a quarter. If I go again, it'll be two and a half years. That would probably be enough to catch it. Neuter it, before it got its claws in. Then I'd have, who knows? Twenty years to live.

Or thirty-five, if I do a Jaclyn. Or I could get run over by a bus next Thursday. Or, if the Pocket takes me forward a year, well.' She shrugged.

The bartender watched her impassively.

'My daughter, Claudie, thinks this is a very bad idea.'

'What do you think?' he said.

She shrugged again. 'I think thinking is over-rated. I think cucumber is a very pointless vegetable. I think I'd like a vodka.' Vodka was supposed to be tasteless anyway, wasn't it? No loss, then.

The bartender poured her an inch of clear, slightly oily-looking liquid over a couple of ice cubes. She brought it to her lips, and wasn't disappointed.

'The problem is,' she said, 'that my life insurance policy has a clause. An addendum. It considers use of the Pocket reckless endangerment. They don't like the odds, you see. So if I go in, and it takes me forward, they'll say that was a deliberate act on my part. I will be the author of my own misfortune. And they'll cut the payout to my beneficiary. My daughter. Claudie feels that would be very unfair.'

The bartender topped up her vodka without being asked. 'What do you feel?'

She looked up at him. Was he a robot? The conversation had that generic quality she associated with telephone switchboards. Would you like to be connected to the complaints department? Can we provide a quote for any of your other insurance needs? I'm sorry, I didn't understand that response.

Did they have robots that sophisticated, nowadays? Maybe. If you could travel in time—well, in a small, localised pocket the size of a cupboard, at least—why couldn't you have robot bartenders, too? It made sense. As much as anything did, anyway.

She patted his hand. It was very firm. And warm. The marvels of modern technology. 'Thank you,' she said.

He smiled. 'You're welcome. I think they're ready for you now.'

Disa looked behind her. The door was open and the receptionist was gesturing for her to come through.

She took her phone out of her bag and checked the display. Fifteen missed calls and ten text messages.

'It'll be best if you leave that here,' the receptionist said. 'The Pocket doesn't tend to be kind to electronic equipment, I'm afraid.'

The calls and messages were all from Claudie. They always were.

'It's all right,' Disa said. She slipped the phone back into her bag and clutched it to her chest. Tucked safely inside, she had her copy of *Twenty-Five Again!* and a deluxe package of crystals, personally energised by Jaclyn Castleton.

'I'm happy to take my chances,' she said, and followed the receptionist out of the room.

The Volcano Keeper

Jenny Wong

Jenny Wong is a writer, traveler, and occasional business analyst. When she's not attempting to use her computer science degree for good, she's writing at home in her loft or out adventuring with her wise-cracking husband and their grumpy middle-aged dog. Her publications include The Quilliad, 3Elements Review, Grain Magazine, Vallum, NōD Magazine, Cha: An Asian Literary Journal, and elsewhere.

The Ujimi pine forest reaches up towards the moon, luring pale light to trickle down between jagged treetops and rest on soft powdered snow. Ari follows no path, wandering around the thickened shadows of trees, bending beneath bristled boughs, searching through this patchwork of light and darkness. The pine cones wait for her to find them. Their heat marks, little smudges of light, growing dimmer in the cold. A few are found without fuss, as it used to be in the old days. Their small oval bodies roll into her open palm, scales flexing against her skin. Others remind her of escape pods whose navigation has gone off course, lost in a foreign landscape of winter whites. For those ones, she must sift through the drifts, find their crash points, and rescue the wooden husks from a bitter fate of frostbite and slow rot.

The pine cones are few this evening, barely enough to half fill the satchel she keeps tucked in her brown cloak. Ari turns home to Mount Panajashi which looms ahead with its rounded peaks, like the head of a woman lying down, uneven mouth opened up to the sky.

The breath of the sleeping volcano is warm and welcoming. Ari navigates the sinuous lava tubes, watching the cold damp rise in a glow of steam from her clothes. Her eyes register frequencies of both light and heat, an unusual trait of her people, so that even in the blackest of caves, she requires no lamp to see. Yet still, she finds herself whispering, "Left for thirty, right for ten, left for twelve, then straight to the end." It was a game they played as children, back when the corridors were filled with the voices and footsteps of her people. They would cover their eyes with strips of cloth and race to see who could navigate the lava tubes the fastest. Some did it by feel, others memorized step combinations, and everyone earned scraped palms and bloody knees as penance for their mistakes.

The Seeding Chamber is a small circular room with a dozen fist-sized holes clustered in the center of the floor, black and open, like baby birds waiting to feed. One by one, Ari plops the pine cones into these smooth small gullets. The cones will continue on, rolling past heated vents, opening up in the simmering subterranean heat, yielding the faint sticky scent of sap and their precious cargo of seeds. Gravity and series of sharp ledges will separate seed from cone. The seeds will slip through narrowing channels until they breach the cave walls and are gathered, warm and naked, into waiting hands. Meanwhile, the spent cones, too big to follow the seeds, will continue on down the rocky path to incineration. In theory. But sometimes, Ari imagines little Hrokai live behind the walls, plucking out the seeds and saving the dry crusty scales to cover their round demon bodies.

After the last of the cones have been sent on their journey, Ari takes a hundred and thirty-three steps forward and is released into the cool night air and the upturned mouth of Mount Panajashi. The main caldera is a gentle sloping dish of fractured rock and cold magma, protected from winds, and open to the stars. The curved walls are terraced, cut with shallow shelves that step right up to the rounded rim. During its greatest time, the caldera was ringed with life, all of the shelves filled with emerald bursts of sprouts and saplings. Now, although seedlings still continue to grow here, many of the rings are empty or incomplete, leaving a sickly imprint reminiscent of an old abandoned rib cage.

Over by the entrance, there is a pattering of raindrop-sized pods against basket walls. The night's seeds have begun to arrive. Once the sounds have ceased, Ari takes the new seeds into her palm, pressing them into soft spaces of soil, whispering an ancient blessing for life and growth. A soft hum tingles in the air as the seedlings huddle in neat nursery rows, pushing down their roots, turning soot and black into soft brushes of green. The ones that survive the winter will be planted once the warming season comes, thickening the blanket of the forest, as was the job of her people since Mount Panajashi's first eruption over a thousand years ago.

With her task done for the night, Ari heads back inside, winding through the volcano's obsidian arteries, to her favorite lookout point, a little alcove tucked high up overlooking the trees. She sits and peers out beyond the forest, where Hjarakhil is growing wider against the horizon. Its artificial edges scraping up the land, bringing the hard blackness of wide streets and the sharp glitter of colossal towers. Most of her people have been swallowed up by Hjarakhil, inhabiting in the throats of the crystal spires whose air was rumored to be so clean it had no scent.

It would only be a few more seasons until the odorless towers of Hjarakhil would reach the majestic trees of Mount Panajashi. And then, Ari wondered, what would happen? Would anyone remember that only the root song of the Ujimi pines could convince Mount Panajashi to continue in her slumber?

A wind gust blows long and hard against the volcano's side, sending a murky tone shivering along the corridors. She knows that sound, that single note of lonely song. The Barren Storms are coming, with their shrill howls and daggers of ice that threaten to fray the edges of the forest. Ari places a palm down beside her, feels the gentlest of trembles in the rock, the stirrings of consciousness rising closer and closer to the surface.

Time and Space

Laine Perez

Laine Perez teaches composition and literature at North Arkansas College. She received her Ph.D.in English from the University of Texas at Austin. Her work has appeared in Glint Literary Journal and Broad! Literary Journal.

1.

When Mira sees the library for the first time, it is exactly as she remembers it.

It's not much to look at, but it's still nice that this facility has one. Mira's second facility had a dance studio and the first one had a greenhouse, but this is her first with a library.

Most of the chairs in the room are by the windows offering a glimpse of the garden where the first of the corn has begun to ripen. Mira lies between the shelves because this is where she will be when she meets Cy. She reads the first chapters of books and then draws pictures in them, composing landscapes above titles and leaving flowers in the margins.

She draws and waits for Cy to arrive and then she does and Mira remembers all the parts of Cy she had forgotten.

Cy spreads herself out into a room, and it gladly accommodates her, her low tuneless hum embedding itself in the floorboards and her heavy step imprinting in the rafters.

"Hello," she says, and Mira looks up. Cy's face is soft, rounded and fuzzy around the edges. It is a face designed to be touched.

She cranes her neck to look at the picture Mira has drawn: a cabin surrounded by tall pines.

"Huh," she says. She kneels on the floor to get a better look. "Are you defacing books?" she asks.

Speech has always come to Mira slowly. She does not find an answer before Cy's body lurches fiercely to the left.

"Oh," she says and disappears.

This is not unexpected. Mira crawls into the space Cy abandoned and pulls over her book to finish her picture.

2.

It was supposed to be a secret, but everyone could see who returned the orange form at the beginning of the term and who didn't. So everyone in Mira's class knew about Clarissa's and Violet's oddities. There was considerable speculation about what they could do. A girl in the grade ahead of them could change the color and shape of almost anything. Tomas's sister could create light.

Clarissa made it snow on a warm afternoon in October.

When she came back to school, Hannah Rios asked her what it felt like.

Clarissa shrugged. "Nothing," she said.

Mira found this answer disappointing. It should have felt like someone grabbing her head with both hands and wrenching it around.

But perhaps seeing the future was different from creating weather.

Mira's oddity had developed in the spring. It began with three second glimpses: a bird taking flight, a pencil dropping, a door closing once and then again. The visions slowly grew in duration.

Mira thought about telling her mom, but when her mom came home from work, her body was always a long, drooping line, so Mira said nothing.

In August, when she brought home the orange form, she folded it into a swan, and gave it to her mom who put it on the kitchen counter. Her mom made a sign and taped it next to the fragile paper bird. It read, "Swan in Orange by Miranda."

"Now everyone will know that it's art," she said.

Two weeks later, Violet turned her desk into a block of ice.

Mira told her mom about it, describing how the ice grew, thickening rapidly as it sped down the sides of the desk. Within fifteen minutes, the creation was complete. Once Violet was removed, the desk began to drip, the ice fracturing under the sunlight.

Her mom shivered and then reached out to hold Mira close. "Isn't it good," she said, "not to have to worry about any of that?"

Mira agreed.

3.

In the library, a stack of books waits for Mira. A note hides inside the book on the top of the stack. Cy has written "if you are going to deface books, at least choose ones that no one (beside me) will read."

This gift deserves acknowledgement. She spends her days a satellite in Cy's orbit and plans the words she will say, rolling the shape of them across her tongue.

Late in the afternoon on a Tuesday, they are outside in the garden picking corn, moving slowly through the rows, bound by the humidity and heat.

Cy says, "Did I scare you? Some people really don't know how to take it. My disappearing act."

Mira shakes her head.

"Okay. That's good." She reaches for the next stalk. "So, I was reading a book, and I found one of your pictures. I'd like to find more. So, I figured if I knew where to look—" She glances at Mira. "But you don't have to use them. The books. Unless you want."

"I do," Mira says. "It's good. Thank you." These words are feeble. They are not the ones she had planned.

Cy nods. "Yeah. Okay," she says. "You're welcome."

She tosses an ear of corn down into the basket, and Mira leans into her, close enough to see her freckles and the soft dark hair on her cheeks and the beads of sweat at her temples. Cy doesn't move away. She closes her eyes and waits. A strand of hair is sticking to her forehead. Mira takes the hair between two fingers and tucks it into her braid. Before she can lower her hand, Cy claims it. She squeezes once and leads Mira on to the next row.

4.

Unexpectedly, Mira's mom died.

Mira went to live with Amelia, her mom's best friend. Amelia lived in the country. She had land and a two-story house and a garden and chickens and bees.

Mira was welcome to help with the chickens and the garden if she wanted or to wander around the property if she wanted or stay in her room if she wanted. She did not have to eat or sleep or talk and if all she wanted to do was watch TV or sit outside in the grass and do nothing that was okay.

Mira did not want to do anything for a long time.

On Thursdays, Amelia's neighbor Martin came for dinner. He always brought a jar of jam which Amelia spooned out into a glass dish and placed on the table. Their conversation plodded comfortably in familiar quiet circles. When new material entered, it was handled carefully, talked around rather than through.

"They finished that facility," Martin said. "The one for the girls—the odd ones."

"Well, they've been working on it for a while," Amelia said.

"I guess they don't have to go to Texas anymore," Martin said.

"I guess not," Amelia said.

"Lita's oldest asked to go," Martin said. "They never did find where she sent that TV."

Amelia nodded. "I guess she figures they can help."

"Maybe they can," Martin said.

"Maybe," Amelia said. "And maybe she doesn't need help."

"Maybe so," Martin said.

Amelia didn't know about Mira's oddity. So, Mira told her.

"Okay," Amelia said. "Have you thought about what you would like for dinner?"

In the waning days of the summer, Amelia taught her how to

repot a plant, and Martin taught her how to make jam. Mira went back to school and learned that she was both ahead of and behind her classmates. To help, Amelia brought home books from the library. Mira didn't read them, but she liked to see the stack of them next to her bed.

She liked the farm and she liked Amelia and she liked Martin, but she kept seeing visions of herself in a small, sparsely furnished blue room.

In December, Amelia took her to the facility.

"If you want to come back, you just have to call," she said.

She would not come back to Amelia's house again, but there was no reason to tell Amelia this. The choice was made, and it couldn't be undone.

The little blue room was exactly as she had seen it.

5.

Mira's yellow rain jacket is old and heavy, and she is already sweating by the time she reaches the dining hall.

Cy is sitting at a table by the door. When Mira drops into a seat next to her, she laughs.

"What's this?" she asks, her hands plucking at the jacket. "You know something I don't?"

Mira could answer yes, but Cy will ask questions, and that isn't the way this is supposed to go. They won't talk until after, and in-between there will be a long period where they don't talk at all.

She shrugs.

"It's too big for you," Cy says. She places one of Mira's arms on the table and begins rolling up the sleeve. Mira remembers watching Cy's hands fold the fabric over and over, so she knows to wrap her fingers tight around Cy's when Cy's body jerks away from her.

They disappear, and it is easy, like slipping out of one room and into another.

In the new place, it is raining like Mira knew it would be. She takes off her jacket and tries to give it to Cy. She doesn't take it. She says, "We have to get back. And you should put your coat back on. You're getting soaked."

Mira lets the jacket hang off the ends of her fingers. Cy turns and walks up the street. Mira follows. She tries to drape the jacket over Cy's shoulders. Cy bats her away.

"You should have asked," Cy says, "if you could come."

Mira doesn't know how to explain that she couldn't have asked, but it doesn't matter anyway because Cy isn't listening, and the ugly part is coming.

"You just invaded," Cy says. "Like you belonged." Her expression twists, and the knowable grooves and planes of her face become frightening in their unfamiliarity. "You don't belong here, and you shouldn't have come."

"I'm sorry," Mira says, but Cy has already turned away.

Later, when they are on a bus, Mira falls asleep, and when she wakes, her head is lolling against Cy's shoulder, and Cy's fingers are untangling knots from her hair. She is not particularly gentle, but she also hasn't forgiven Mira yet.

It takes hours to get home. Mira's scalp aches for two days.

6.

The facility promised control.

"But," Dr. Davis said, "proper discipline must be applied."

She handed Mira a small notebook. Inside, the pages were lined with columns. There was a column labeled "Days and Times" and one labeled "Physical Sensations." The column labeled "Description of Occurrence" included a note: "proper completion of this section might require the assistance of others."

The other doctor, Dr. Gates, proposed changes to their diets and daily exercise and meditation. He had them study less and spend more hours outside growing flowers and climbing trees. He gave them jobs around the facility and talked to each of them about how they were feeling and asked if they were happy.

Mira wasn't happy or unhappy. Her visions came when they liked just as they always had. She began seeing herself in a place where it snowed in the winter.

The year she turned eighteen, since she wasn't showing much progress, Dr. Gates gave her the option to leave. "You can go home," he said. "Or to another facility. One that isn't concerned with... resolving your oddity."

Or, Dr. Davis said, she could stay. She told Mira that she was certain that she could still find a mechanism for control. "So, you won't have to worry anymore," she said.

Dr. Gates said, "It's up to you, Mira."

It wasn't, not really, so on the first warm day in spring, Mira went north.

7.

Mira is nearly asleep when Cy comes into her room. Cy stands with her back against the door, and Mira isn't sure that she is real until she says, "Did you know I was going to disappear?"

Mira sits up. "Yes."

"Because you knew you would come with me?" Cy asks.

"Yes," Mira says.

"Do we go anywhere else?" Cy asks.

"Lots of places," Mira says.

Cy perches on the end of the bed. "Where?"

"I don't know," Mira says. "I thought you would know."

"I never know where I'm going to end up," Cy says.

"How does it work?" Mira asks.

Cy shrugs. "Sometimes I think of a place, remember a place, and then I'll be there. Sometimes I can remember without going anywhere."

Mira moves over closer to the wall, leaving space for Cy. "It's late," she says. Cy lays down.

"Why do you come back?" Mira asks.

"Where else would I go?" Cy asks.

"Anywhere," Mira says.

"Why do you stay?" Cy asks.

"I won't," Mira says. "Not for much longer."

"But you stay here. You came here," Cy says.

"Yes," Mira says.

"Why?" Cy asks.

"Because I knew I would meet you here," Mira says.

"Oh," Cy says.

"We should sleep," Mira says.

She doesn't sleep well. She is too hot and does not have enough space, but, in the morning, Cy is still next to her, soundly asleep, hands fisted in the sheets, and it feels like she's always been there.

8.

It did snow at the next facility, and the winter was very cold.

Mira arrived in the spring. Her roommate, Sonia, had the bed by the air conditioner. "But you can have it if you want," she said. Mira declined and took the bed by the door.

Sonia, Mira knew, created heat. It boiled up from under her skin, and once it became unbearable, she stripped down to her underwear and lay on the floor. She kept ice packs in a freezer by her bed. Mira placed them on her forehead, under her arms, and on the back of her neck.

The winter was better. Sonia climbed out the window and curled up in the snow. She was frozen when she came back inside, soaked in water and sweat, and Mira untangled her from her clothing and wrapped her in the extra blanket from the closet.

She asked Mira to come with her when she left. Mira liked Sonia. She liked having someone to take care of.

She also knew she would never go further north than she was.

Mira stayed.

9.

Mira and Cy travel. Some places they leave quickly and some they linger in. When they return, no one seems to remember that they have been gone.

Cy's stuff moves into Mira's room. Cy sometimes occupies the side of the bed closest to the wall.

They are alone in the dark quiet before morning when Cy says, "You knew you would meet me. You saw me. You saw us together."

"Yes," Mira says.

"So, is that why we're together? Because you saw me? Is that why you chose me?"

"You chose. I didn't," Mira says.

Cy shifts to look at Mira.

"I saw you talk to me in the library. I saw us travel together," Mira says. "You let me be with you. You chose. I just went to the right place at the right time."

"What if I hadn't done any of those things?" Cy asks.

"I wouldn't have seen them," Mira says.

"And we never would have met?" Cy asks.

Mira nods.

"So, I chose?" Cy says.

"Yes," Mira says.

Cy rolls on to her back. "But you had to choose me too."

"I suppose," Mira says though she never thinks of anything she does as choosing. She does what she sees herself doing, but this is difficult to explain.

Cy wraps her hand loosely around Mira's wrist, binding Mira to her. After she falls asleep, Mira gently detaches herself.

10.

The morning after Etta moved into Mira's room, a large flowering plant sprouted up from between the floorboards. The next morning a series of dandelions appeared. It was buttercups after that and then a tall leafy weed. Etta cleaned off her shoes before she came inside, but the plants still came.

"I can't grow them from nothing," she said. "The seeds must have already been there. I'm sorry."

Mira didn't mind. Before Etta had arrived, Mira had built a little flower box for their window. Together they pulled up whatever had grown in the night and planted it in the dark, fresh soil.

Etta avoided going outside when she could help it, but Mira knew that when she asked, Etta would come out with her. The night she chose was warm and dry. Mira brought a blanket, and they sat in the meadow beyond the facility. Etta fell asleep first. Mira woke to soft colors, the smell of wildness, and Etta's laughter. She had woven flowers into Mira's hair in the early hours of morning. "You look awful," she said. "I did a terrible job." Mira pulled up long blades of grass and bundles of purple and white flowers and bound them together, placing them into Etta's arms.

Mira knew Etta would not stay long. She woke up on the first day of September to Etta's hands tucking a daisy behind her ear. She said, "I have to go home." Mira nodded. Etta left Mira her address and her phone number and invited her to come and stay for a little while or for longer, but Mira would not call or write or visit.

For the first time, Mira was by herself in the little room. It felt larger and then smaller and then she had visions of a girl with dark hair and freckles who was kind to her.

So, Mira left.

11.

Mira takes only her yellow raincoat on the day of her final departure. Cy sees the coat and immediately packs a small grey bag. It looks heavy. Mira doesn't ask what's in it.

Cy holds tight to the bag in her left hand and clings to Mira with her right when they disappear.

It's not raining when they arrive in the woods, but the air is damp, and it smells like pine.

"There's a cabin," Cy says. "Up the path a bit."

The first of the rain starts to fall once they reach the porch. Cy pulls a key out of her bag and unlocks the door. Inside it is dark and filled with dust, so they leave the door open and sit outside. Cy's hair curls at the ends. Mira takes off her shoes and settles her feet against the railing.

"You're going back soon," Mira says.

"Maybe," Cy says. "Maybe not."

This is unexpected. Something small and fragile flutters its paper-thin wings in the cavity between Mira's heart and lungs. But then she remembers. Cy does not know what Mira knows. Cy can speak as if there are uncertainties. Mira has seen herself in the cabin alone. She has not yet seen how Cy will leave her, but the leaving is inevitable. This is how it always happens.

"You could come with me," Cy says. "If I do go."

Mira thinks for a long time. She knows she will not see this option. She knows, and she knows. Yet, still, she curls her fingers around Cy's wrist.

"Yes," she says.

The rain lasts almost an hour. They sit outside until the dusk leeches all the color out of the landscape. Then, finally, they go inside.

Campfire Songs

Kimberly Rei

When I was five years old, my parents gave me a set of Children's Classics. I couldn't yet read them, but I remember being giddy with the potential. That Christmas launched my love of words. I've been writing and reading for as long as I can remember. I am fortunate to live in gorgeous Florida with my wondrous wife, where beaches and crisp sunlight inspire me daily. It is entirely on me that sunlight rarely makes it into my stories.

The woods grew darker as the sun slipped behind the horizon. This meant that maybe the howling band that chased me would drift off in search of easier prey. But it also meant howling creatures of another kind were just starting to stir. Everything was howling and hungry these days, it seemed. There was a good chance I had sealed my fate running past the tree line, but I'd rather take my chances with wolves. They only ate your flesh.

I kept moving in the hopes of finding something I could set my back against. An empty cave would be perfect, but a tight crop of trees might work. I had learned as a child how to move swiftly over just about any terrain, so I dodged roots and bushes with ease. A patch of slick mud nearly took me down and I slammed a shoulder into a large trunk. I would feel that later.

A fresh howl broke out behind me. Far too close for comfort, the howl sent me pounding over roots and leaves once more, a fresh burst of terror giving me speed. I glanced over my throbbing shoulder and when I turned back, the trees had opened to a clearing. Voices. I heard someone talking! They didn't seem to care who heard them. Were they fools? Moving too fast to skid to a halt, I braced myself for the burst of pain that came with a drop-and-roll behind a rusted-out car. The distant voices drew closer. I couldn't let myself be seen. Not until I knew who they were. What they were. My gaze flicked around, frantic. This car wouldn't hide me for long.

A neat row of decrepit houses stood a good dash away. They'd been bombed and looted, but one near the middle seemed to have survived. Most of the windows were unbroken. The front door hung by one hinge, which was a hinge more than the others. The house stood at least three floors high, with what looked like an attic. There was a chance it was inhabited, but if so, no one was moving around inside.

The voices grew louder. It was now or never. My shoulder twinged as I pushed off the rusty beast and ran, dust kicking up behind me. There was no help for that. I could only hope the people coming this way would not notice my footprints. Checking my pace, I ducked through the door and pressed against the first wall I found. It is a skill to keep from panting when you are scared and desperate for breath. You must breathe in slowly through your nose, out gently through your mouth. Slow the heart rate and the breath. Remain silent. Listen.

Nothing. Could this place truly be abandoned? Or were the inhabitants returning home even now?

As quickly and carefully as I knew how, I ran up all the stairs and I didn't stop until I reached a solid looking door at the top. The layer of dust on the handle said it hadn't been used in years. If anyone came after me, one glance at that knob and the smeared dirt would give me away. Still, it was a chance I had to take if I wanted to hide, even for a night. No sane soul dared go unsheltered at night.

Dim light came through the window as I opened the door, then closed it behind me. My eyes widened in wonder. Was that a bed? A real bed? It was small, as if meant for a child, but not so small that I couldn't rest there. A dresser and a smaller desk with a great big mirror attached to it was nearby a cushioned seat. Shelf after shelf graced the walls, filled with toys. It was as if the war's destruction had left this room entirely alone. As if the fallout didn't matter, the bands of desperate people didn't exist. As if I had stepped into a place forgotten by truth.

I sat on the bed and nearly wept. It would take a day or two, maybe more, to be sure this house wasn't taken. But if my luck held out, I might have a new home!

A full moon rose slowly, glowing red as ever, but for the first time in a long time, I was not afraid. I was too intrigued. I no longer heard the voices and there seemed to be no movement at all in the house, so I wandered the room freely, picking up various objects and turning them over in my hand. The hairbrush didn't do much for my short tangle, but it was still fun to use. After all, I hadn't seen one in more than a decade. A delicate beaded bracelet fell apart in my hands when I picked it up, scattering tiny bits of colour across the wood floor and into the throw rugs. I trailed my fingers over the shelves, marveling that they still hung so straight and strong.

And that's when I saw her. A pretty little doll, the size of a newborn babe. She had a blue and white checked dress and little blue shoes. There was even lace on her white socks. How had they stayed so clean? I was afraid to touch her and make her dirty, but her blond hair looked so soft, I couldn't resist. I picked her up carefully and stroked that hair, playing with the curls. She was beautiful enough to move me to tears.

As I ran my fingers through the silken yellow, one caught on a plastic ring and I tried to yank my hand away. A cheerful voice filled the room, "Hello! I'm Cathy! What's *your* name?"

I almost dropped her. What trickery was this? Was she a spy's tool? A radio? Was there a camera in those little eyes? I shook her. I turned her over and over, looking for proof. Nothing.

My name. What was my name? I hadn't thought of myself by a name in a very long time. And what if I answered her? Would she respond? I nibbled my cracked lip and took a chance, "I'm... I'm Sura. It's nice to meet you, Cathy."

Again, nothing. No response. If she was a plant, she was a sneaky one. Or maybe whoever had set her up had long since left their post. What if she was meant to help? She might have clues about this place.

I pulled the string again.

"Please take me with you."

I wasn't expecting that. Not these words or the shift in tone. The cheerfulness was gone, replaced by need. The hairs on the back of my neck started to rise. In any other circumstance, I would have listened and gotten out of there. But I needed to know more before I left this potential haven.

I pulled the string again. The doll shuddered in my hands. "Run, Sura. Run NOW!"

I ran. Down the stairs and out the front door, for once not caring who heard me. Survival instinct of a more primal nature took over. It wasn't until I was halfway between the rusted-out car and the tree line that I paused for a breath.

That was when I noticed the doll was still in my hands. I nearly threw her from me, but something made my hand tighten instead. More of that instinct. I turned to look at the house and dropped to my knees, cradling Cathy against me. Red eyes blinked from the top window. One pair. Then another. More and more until the glass was nearly full of crimson winking on and off. I'd never seen anything like it. But Cathy had lived with it. She lived with them. I knew then that she had saved me. Leaving her behind wasn't going to be an option.

I shifted, holding her a little more gracefully. Night had fallen, leaving only the red moonglow. It didn't look like the eyes were planning to come after us. That left other, more immediate concerns to tend. I hadn't slept rough since my childhood and I didn't want to dust those skills off now. Unfortunately, this was fairly new territory to me. I'd been through once or twice before, but never long enough to get a good feel for the lay of the land. The loss of the house still stung and oddly clouded my ability to consider other options. I wanted to go back and stretch out in that clean bed. More than anything, I wanted to recapture that fleeting sensation that everything was going to be okay. The truth threatened to drag me down and under.

On a whim, I tugged the doll's cord, "Well? You got any bright ideas?"

"Auntie."

My grip tightened, and I stared into her glass eyes, "What did you say?"

Silence. I cursed whoever designed this puzzle and pulled the string, harder this time as if that might power her for more than one answer.

"Ow! Auntie. We must find Auntie."

My head filled with a tumble of questions, but there wasn't time to ask any of them. The only idea worse than finding Auntie was staying out here much longer. The moon was reaching its peak, bringing with it the kind of night life best avoided. The howling started up again, far behind us. Not far enough if I could still hear it.

"Auntie. Tiny gods, doll, you do ask a lot."

I tucked her under my arm and took off at a ground-eating lope, leaning forward just enough to let my weight give me speed. It was an old trick that left you more tired at the end of the journey, but it helped ensure you'd arrive at all. My people had learned many ways to survive. A few had even been passed down to me.

Getting to Auntie wasn't the problem. Her lair was well-known, at the center of one of the permanent camps. A small town running on theft and barter had sprung up around her, paying homage in both cash and respect. No one knew where Auntie came from, but we all knew her role, even when we didn't know our own. Getting in to see her was the real trouble. Especially for me.

"You. You're banned, waif."

I wheezed, gasping for air. The run had taken more out of me than anticipated.

The rather large man blocking the doorway chuckled, "Best go back the way you came before she catches your scent. You remember what she said about seeing your face again?"

I nodded. I wasn't likely to forget so creative a death threat. One final wheeze and my voice crept back into my throat, "I have to risk it, Merry."

He chortled and shook his head, then stepped aside, "There might be enough left of you to keep the shades from our door tonight. Got anything of worth I should strip from your corpse?"

I ignored him and stepped into the maze of tents. In most places, the cloth rose high enough to stand upright, but every now and then, I had to duck as I moved through the darkness. Muscle memory carried me to Auntie's chamber. The delicate lick of incense rewarded my instinct and turned my stomach. This was going to be rough.

I moved out of darkness and into flickering light. There were enough candles in this cloth suite to read by, more than enough for Auntie to recognize me the instant I entered the room. I blinked, pretending light blindness and trying to buy myself a moment.

Auntie sat on a raised dais, lounging against a pile of silk and velvet pillows. There were enough to craft an impressive and cozy throne perched high to let long legs stretch and give her the air of a ruler. She was as close to royalty as the deadlands dared claim. I glanced at her, brushing my gaze quickly to drink in her mood. People lived and died by what Auntie was wearing on any given day. My stomach clenched.

Those long legs were encased in loose black pants that tightened as they climbed her form until they hugged high on her waist and gave way to a shirt more white than it had any right to be. It was a mystery of the lands how she managed to keep anything so pristine. I had a flash of the lace on the doll's socks. That same white. Auntie's pleated shirt vanished into a flowing black jacket with darted sleeves spilling over the wildly coloured pillows. An ominous claret scarf hung around her neck.

I dared to look up.

A top hat of respectable splendour rested on a waterfall of midnight blue hair. Had it been any other time, I would have clapped at the sight of such a perfect appearance. She looked phenomenal. Of course, I was ignoring the reason she wanted my head on a pike.

Auntie's voice flowed toward me, the tone deep and masculine and knotted with menace, "I never took you for a Fool, waif. Daring, perhaps, but never foolish."

Her voice froze what was left of hope. Auntie managed her world by never settling into one of anything. She was never entirely she, nor entirely he, though always She if you knew what was good for you. Only a cherished few knew exactly what lay beneath her elaborate costumes. As a gift to all of us, she used her appearance and persona as a warning of her moods. It would seem she had known I was coming. I wondered what method Merry used to inform her so swiftly.

She raised a filigree silver talon and stroked over the vicious scar that lived where an eye should. Puckered flesh was cut through with a red line that never seemed to lose its angry glow. I winced.

"Gives me a roguish air, does it not? Should I thank you, waif?"

"No, Auntie."

"Ah! It speaks. Then perhaps it can explain why it hauled its infernal hide back into my presence?"

The pattern of her words never shifted, but I could hear the fury in each casual syllable. I wanted to throw myself at her feet and beg her forgiveness. But if it hadn't worked when I accidentally took her eye, it certainly wouldn't work now.

"I found something of interest."

The silence stretched. She stared at me as if I had lost my mind. Nothing shy of another apocalypse should have brought me to her door and here I was, seemingly offering a tinker's bobble.

She shifted and held out a hand. I eased forward and gave her the doll. Her voice rose several octaves as she gently took my prize. She cradled it to her chest and leaned back, eyes closed against powerful emotion. "Where did you find this?"

"In an abandoned house. The room at the very top. It was perfect, Auntie! I swear, time forgot to pass there."

"Yes. It would. By the tiny gods, how did you manage to bring her to me?"

I shook my head, confused. "I just picked her up."

"Did she speak to you?"

"She told me to run."

Auntie rose and stepped down to glare at me. She was taller than I remembered. Or maybe I just felt terribly small.

"How? She only speaks to yetemeret'u ."

"The Chosen? Auntie! Is that... am I... am..." my voice stuck as the weight of that one word settled on my shoulders.

Auntie burst into laughter, the sound sinking into the cloth tent walls, "No, idiot. Yetemeret'u was born eight cycles ago. This doll was her protector."

She folded herself onto the floor, legs crossed, and motioned for me to do the same. I obeyed, grateful I had seemingly done something right. I might survive this night after all. Merry was going to have to find another sacrifice for the shades.

"Guardian. What happened?" Auntie held the doll on her lap, looking into the blue glass eyes.

I reached for the plastic ring, "I had to pull this to make her talk."

The slap rang loud and carried a sharp sting. I snatched my hand back, giving Auntie a wounded look.

"Foolish waif. Be silent and learn. Guardian. Will you speak with me?"

"Of course, Holy One."

I found a spot on the rug to stare at, deliberately not responding outwardly to the honourific. I could feel Auntie staring at me, waiting for me to chew on my foot. The moment stretched out. Finally, Auntie turned her attention back to the doll.

"What happened to the child? What happened to your defenses?"

Cathy was silent for so long, I thought she'd shut down or was refusing to tell the tale. Her porcelain body shuddered and if she hadn't been a doll, I would have said she sagged in Auntie's grip. Her head lifted, and she turned to stare at the blank cloth wall.

The wall transformed from tent to stone. A bright room stretched further and wider than the current space. The marble fountain happily burbling was the same pristine white as the floors and walls. Matching columns broke the space up into a bathing area, an open closet, a play room, and a bedroom with a massive, raised bed. I could swim in that fluffy comforter and sleep like the dead against the silk pillows piled high. A young girl sat in the middle of the bed, stark and gorgeous. She was almost too thin, but it made her look ethereal rather than scrawny. She wore a silk froth of a dress, just as white as the rest of the room. Her hair fell in equally pale waves, pooling around her. When she moved, there was an abalone shimmer to the strands. Her skin, though, was the most glorious deep ebony, drinking in the light and tossing it back gently. Leaf green eyes, bright and nearly mythic in shade, danced as she chattered away to Cathy.

A door to the right opened and several men burst into the room. They were covered head to toe in deep crimson cloth, only their eyes showing. The tallest grabbed the child and clamped a hand over her mouth. She thrashed and clawed at him, but he simply tucked her under his arm like a sack.

"Disable that thing!"

Another man aimed a hand at Cathy. His palm glowed then flared with an overly-bright blue flash. The vision shivered and began to fade. Before it winked out completely, I hear the tall man snarl again, "Bring it along. It's more obvious left behind."

I started to ask what happened after that when the image returned. My words shifted on their way up my throat, "That's the room! That's where I found Cathy!"

Another slap, this time to the back of my head. But it was true. The same skinny bed, the same dresser, the same desk and mirror. And the same shelves. Both the child and the doll sat on the bed, but the girl wasn't chattering. She was staring out of the window, her leaf green eyes dull and saddened. I wanted to step into the scene and wrap her up in a warm embrace.

Cathy didn't look right, either. She wasn't speaking or moving at all. Her eyes were locked and vacant. Clearly she was recording, but whatever her other skills, she couldn't access them. She was as helpless to protect the child as I was.

I tensed as the door opened, quietly this time. The men had returned. My hands curled into fists and I willed myself to stay still and silent. There was nothing I could do but bear witness. And so I would, in every detail.

They wore the same crimson uniforms. Only the tall man stood out as different from the others. Both his height and body shape marked him, and I vowed I would never forget him. I had nowhere to go with my ferocity, but it would help keep me warm.

The tall man lifted the child again. She didn't fight this time. She hung limp when he tossed her over his shoulder.

"Straighten up in here. Make it look like it's been empty. Leave the doll. No one who finds it will know what it is. Damn thing will explode if we cause it too much harm. Last one took out two units."

He left with the child. His men smoothed the bed and tucked Cathy onto a shelf where she sat, still unmoving. Once again, the vision faded. Nothing followed.

Auntie straightened, "Well then. I don't suppose you learned anything while you sat there in limbo?"

Cathy chuckled and it was an odd sound. Part grating, part liquid, and part actual amusement. As if she had either been inhaling fog years or had forgotten how to laugh.

"I did, actually. There are creatures hunting her. They came sniffing around after dark. I could not make out much more than red eyes."

I trembled.

Auntie nodded and rose, lifting the doll. She set Cathy on a table beside her pillow throne, "I don't know what those are, but I know your crimson-clad thieves. And I know what that bright flash was. I can protect you against it."

Cathy was silent and I had to bite my lip. All this was going far too slow. I wanted action. I wanted to save the child and be the hero! If I wasn't yetemeret'u, I could rescue her. They would sing songs of me around campfires and I would be welcome at every outpost. I sighed into the vision and earned another slap to the back of my head.

"You should be listening instead of dreaming, waif."

I didn't bother wondering how she knew. Auntie always knew. I refocused half-way through a sentence.

"...where we can find a former Kith. He may even know what the creatures are or where they came from. He's deep in hiding. No one leaves the Kith. But I have a chit I can call in. I assume you'll travel with my people to speak with him?"

"I would prefer to, yes."

My mouth got away from me, "I want to go, too!"

I ducked just in time.

Auntie actually laughed, "You truly are a Fool. No, waif, you're going to the training camps."

My heart fluttered and hope, that thing I had been squashing for so many years, stirred in my ribs, "I am?"

Auntie smiled. She reached up to the horrible scar covering her missing eye. Guilt lashed at me again. Her filigree talon stroked the puckered flesh. She watched me for a long moment, silent, then slipped that talon under her skin and peeled it away. I clamped both hands over my mouth to smother a scream. Auntie laughed again, but kept pulling until the scarred, ugly, and apparently fake, flesh tore away. I was expecting to see blood and tissue and a gaping hole. Instead, her skin was smooth and perfect and both eyes blinked at me.

"You had the courage to come after me when you thought I had wronged you. You stood your ground when you thought you'd blinded me. Then you had the courage to come back, knowing the price you would pay. You have spirit, girl. If we can beat some sense into you, we might make some use of you. If you're willing, Merry will take you to the training camps and we'll see."

I wanted to argue and beg to accompany Cathy. I had found her, after all. Surely I had a right to see this through. What about the campfire songs? But sense rose to cover all the whining.

"Thank you, Auntie. I won't let you down."

And that, waifs, is how I came to be here. Now, what's your story?

The Thing In the Walls Wants Your Small Change

Virginia M Mohlere

Virginia M. Mohlere was born on one
solstice, and her sister was born on the
other. Her chronic writing disorder
stems from early childhood. She lives
in the swamps of Houston and writes
with a fountain pen that is extinct in the
wild. Her work has been seen in Cicada,
Lakeside Circus, Journal of Unlikely
Coulrophobia, Strange Horizons, and
Mythic Delirium, among others. This
story is for tumblr user iguanamouth.

The penny was gone again.

Caro huffed and dropped her grocery bags in the hall. She reached in, took a penny from the change bowl by the door, and rubbed it between her thumb and forefinger, said Nana's charm for the house spirits, to keep them happy and home.

She blew on the penny and tucked it down by the threshold.

Five days she'd lived here, and seven times the penny had been gone, either in the morning or after she returned from an errand. The apartment didn't set off her Spooky Senses, but the penny thing was weird.

Nana was unsympathetic.

"Girl, you got house spirits with expensive taste," she said, laughing. "That's what you get, moving yourself where everything's snow and concrete. Down here the house spirits know us. They miss you."

"Nana. That's you missing me," Caro said, guilt eating at her just a tiny bit.

Just a tiny bit: mostly, she was still pinching herself that everything had worked out so smoothly: this cute little apartment with southern exposure, high tin ceilings, and a dark-stained, carved sideboard set into the dining/living room wall that she loved so much she wanted to lie down on top of it despite its sticking drawers. This ridiculous neighborhood that was like something out of a romantic comedy, with its painfully adorable coffee shops, blocks of grey stone townhouses, and ethnic restaurants entirely outside the dreams of most other people from Pointe Coupee Parish.

And the job. Hired from across the dang country to write cyber-security algorithms for enough money that the offer letter had made her choke, when surely there were a thousand coders nearby who'd have jumped at the chance. After 2 weeks, she still half expected that to show up at the address every morning and find an empty lot. It was too hard to believe this was all real.

"Yes, it's me missing you, baby. Every old minute. But you know I'm happy for you."

"I know, Nana."

"Your mama keeps asking after you."

And there was the familiar sensation of acid boiling up into her sternum.

"Nana, you won't –"

"I won't, baby. I won't ever give her your number, I promise. I do keep telling her you're happy as can be."

Caro laughed.

"That must make her furious."

Nana laughed too, but high-pitched, tense.

"That it does. Don't you let that snake I birthed hurt you all that way away. You go to your fancy job and show them how lucky they are to have you, and call me on the iPad on Sunday so I can see your face."

"Love you Nana."

"Love you, baby."

The penny was gone again in the morning. Caro rolled her eyes and put another one down.

It was the biggest mystery of her new life in Chicago – which, as troubles go, she was not going to complain about. It wasn't like an extra half-dollar or so each month to appease her greedy house ghost was going to crack her budget, but it vexed her.

Well. And there was that scratchy sound behind the wall in the back hallway, next to the bathroom.

"No way, I spray once a season," her landlord said. "Sorry, kid, it's just an old building. It makes noises."

Which was okay.

"It's rats in the walls. Every building has them. Anybody ever tell you about the super-rats from the eighties? They were the size of cats. My cousin knew a family whose dog got killed by one."

This not-okay statement solidified Troy from sales as The Office Asshole. Poor guy, he seemed so shocked when his follow-up invitation for shots after work got shot down. Ha ha.

Still: rats. Was there anything more gross than rats? Every time she heard that faint scritch behind the wall it made her spine feel like a spaghetti noodle. Was it enough to give up the sideboard?

Was it enough to give up her three-block walk to the train? Or the taco stand two doors down?

She stood in the hallway, staring down at the wall panel, waiting. Wasted *hours* this way, it was so stupid.

It was easy to spend long days at work, avoiding her apartment and the scritch. It was easy to take long walks on weekends. She found an endless supply of cute boutiques and tasty stuff to eat. She learned her way around St. Bran's so thoroughly that she was almost grateful to the scritch for driving her outside.

Her neighbors in the other five apartments were a quiet bunch – she almost never saw them, other than brief greetings at the mailbox or holding the front door open. Seemed like maybe two couples, a guy her age, an older woman, and someone on the third floor who listened to a lot of classical music but never left the building.

Caro found herself in the laundry room with the older woman on a Saturday morning, having just heard a particularly loud, long scratching sound and something almost like a purr.

"Rats?" the woman said in answer to her question.

She frowned with soft eyes, as if thinking hard. When she shook her head, the beads in her long grey dreads clacked.

"No, I can't see rats. It's an old building, sure, but this is a clean place. Protected."

Protected?

Then the woman grinned and squeezed Caro's bicep in a strong grip.

"You'd be more likely to find, I don't know. Borrowers in the walls. Did you ever read that book when you were little? That wouldn't surprise me a bit."

She pulled her clothes – ancient jeans, calico smocks, and faded concert t-shirts – out of the dryer and laughed to herself.

"Borrowers in the walls," the woman said, "that's good. I'm going to use that."

Caro shrugged after her.

It made her feel better, though, that her neighbor couldn't "see" rats. To someone who went to the actual bank to get rolls of pennies for house spirits, it didn't even sound so weird. She looked up Borrowers and wished that her eight-year-old self had read the books. Tiny people in the walls who collected junk and put it to ingenious use. That would've been like holding a piece of Nana's old trailer with her, back in the days before Nana got custody.

Back in the days when she hadn't had any possessions she couldn't sleep in, on, or around without their disappearing into vodka bottles or the garbage or the toilet. So a book wouldn't have lasted long anyhow.

She went so far as to actually speak to the cute girl at the gym, whose name – Aly – even turned out to be cute. The first time they went for drinks, Caro stumbled home drunk enough that when she fumbled emptying her jacket pockets and all her change spilled to the floor, she thought 'screw it' and went to bed.

The change was gone in the morning.

God dang. It had been like seventy cents.

Caro heard the scritch and the little purr-sound and knocked one knuckle sharply into the wall panel. The resulting silence was full. Whatever was frozen on the other side of the wall, possibly praying that she had run into the wall by mistake, was too smart for standard rodentia.

"Hey," she said, "don't get greedy."

The penny by the doorjamb stayed for three days, then disappeared. Caro laughed at the floor, pulled a penny out of the bowl, and said the charm.

"I see how it is," she said to the panel in the back hallway, "you require regular offerings. I get it."

She took to leaving pennies and nickels on the floor around the living room. As long as there was a coin or two hanging around on the floor, the luck penny stayed by the front door.

"See? You've worked things out," Nana laughed into the phone. "Though what a house ghost wants with that much currency I can't imagine."

In October, Caro came down with a bad case of the flu and didn't leave the apartment for eight days straight. Takeout and an emergency drop-off of oatmeal and cans of soup from Aly saved her life, but mostly she lay on the couch, alternately shivering and sweating, wishing she'd ever bothered to buy a cable package or at least a charging cable for her iPad that reached all the way to the couch.

She almost called Aly for a ride to the emergency room on day four when she woke from a nap and hallucinated a small black creature in the middle of the floor, picking up a nickel and running down the hallway.

Still, there was no denying when she woke up later that the nickel was gone.

Caro couldn't blame it on the flu when she woke from a

Saturday-afternoon nap three weeks later and saw it again, sitting by her desk with a penny in each. In each claw.

The thing froze when she inhaled; Caro willed her body to relax and closed her eyes to slits. Her heartbeat was fast as a bird's, but she held herself still, hopefully as if she remained asleep.

The thing blinked its red eyes twice, then looked back down at the pennies it held. It made the purring sound she had twice heard behind the wall.

She figured she could probably hold it in her two cupped palms: it was the size of a kitten, the color of charcoal, with a triangle-shaped head and two greenish horn-things curling over the top.

It was obviously a dragon. The tiniest, cutest, most ridiculous dragon any person could imagine, which Caro was obviously doing, because dragons were obviously imaginary. Except for the part where it held a penny in each forelimb. Except for the part where it shoved both pennies into its pointy little jaw and galloped across the room to the back hallway.

Except for the part where *something* had been taking her loose change for the past three months and scritching behind the wall.

Caro tried to see it again. She left change all over the floor and pretended to take naps almost daily, but though she heard it behind the wall, the little sucker remained elusive. She knocked on the wall once and pitched her voice to be as gentle as possible when she said,

"Hey, it's okay to come out. I won't hurt you."

Silence – and all the coins remained on the floor for a couple of days after.

She learned that value wasn't the creature's priority: it liked pennies best, followed by nickels. Dimes and subway tokens would stay on the floor until they were the only things remaining. She got a Canadian penny among her change once; that was snapped up. It preferred shiny pennies to dull ones.

Emergency life-saving via oatmeal caused Aly to appoint herself Boss Of Caro, which sucked at the gym (so many reps) but had its own advantages, aside from Aly's fundamental cuteness. She pitched enough of a fit when she found out that Caro wasn't going home for Thanksgiving that several of the dudebro lifters glowered in their direction. She arrived outside Caro's building at nine a.m. for the drive out to River Forest. Caro brought a bottle of wine and flowers and tried to treat it as a cultural expedition, eating turkey without any cayenne on it, dressing made of bread instead of rice, and not one oyster on the table.

Caro called Nana during the break between dinner and dessert, when Aly and her dad were setting up trays in front of the football game on TV. If she hadn't been at a stranger's house, Caro would've thrown up on the carpet when Nana answered the phone with their code phrase, "I'm sorry, I don't make donations over the phone, but thank you for calling."

Mama was there.

"You all right, honey?" Aly's mom asked.

Caro took the plates out of her hands and used to walk to the living room to calm herself down.

Over the long Thanksgiving holiday, Caro holed herself up with leftovers from Aly's family dinner and banished all motherly thoughts by trying to draw the dragon out, making a trail of pennies down the hallway that led to a highly polished quarter laid just inside her bedroom door. She turned off all the lights at

8:30 and climbed into bed, wedged among pillows, her blankets swirled around with only one eye uncovered but a clear view of the hall and the doorway.

It was over an hour, easy – more than enough time for her limbs to ache with the desire to sleep. Finally, she heard a creak, a scratch, and a sound that might have been sniffing. The little dragon ran down the hallway and skidded to a stop right in front of her doorway. It was almost impossible to see when it was still – just a shadow in the darkness – but she could hear it sniffing. When it walked forward, she could see its little hunched shape, its tail.

She could hear when it found the stack of pennies just inside the living room.

"Rar!"

Its voice was high-pitched and creaky, almost like a dog's squeaker toy, and it took every drop of Caro's willpower not to laugh at the sound.

"Rar rar!"

And happy Thanksgiving to you too, she thought.

It ran back and forth eight times, carrying the pennies to its home behind her bathroom wall, humming to itself the whole time.

It left the ones closest to her bedroom door for last, standing up on its hind legs in a posture so cute that Caro wanted to curl up into a ball, tilting its head back and forth and sniffing.

"Raaaaar," it hummed softly.

The dragon crept into her room, one foot at a time, peering up at the bed between steps, while Caro held herself completely still.

It stopped in front of the quarter and stared down. Sniffed. Bent to touch the coin with the pointy bit of its face. Did it lick the coin? Caro hoped it licked it.

"Haaaaaa," the little dragon breathed.

It picked up the quarter and put it in its mouth, but the coin dropped to the floor with a clink. The dragon froze, staring at the bed. Caro did her best impersonation of a rock.

After half a dozen breaths, the dragon reached down again and picked up the quarter. It shoved the coin back in its mouth and held it in place with one forelimb, then hobbled out of the room on three legs.

Once it was gone, Caro curled up and put both hands over her face. What even was this? If her life got any cuter she might not survive it.

"A dragon," Nana said the next day, her skepticism so strong it would've curdled the cord on a landline.

"I swear! A dragon the size of a kitten."

"Sweetheart, you sure you didn't drink too much at your friend's house?"

"Nana. I've seen it three times. It's what kept taking my spirit penny! I've been leaving coins out for it for months! I wish I could get a photo of it, you would not believe it."

"I don't believe it, baby."

"Nana," Caro groaned. "How is this any weirder than your spirit pennies and all your red strings with knots in them and that gross jar full of herbs that's as old as me?"

"Don't you bad-mouth my binding jar, it's what keeps your mama from making even more trouble."

"Uh huh. And?"

Caro knew the expression Nana was making back at home – lips pressed together so the places where her pink lipstick had feathered up into the wrinkles around her mouth stood out, eyes narrowed behind her gold-rimmed glasses.

Caro noted a trend toward her own face doing the same thing.

Oops.

"Well. I guess I don't want to call my best grandbaby a crazy person. Are you sure it doesn't mean you any harm?" Nana said finally.

"One hundred percent. It's only interested in money."

Nana laughed.

"Well that's true of lots of folks! You ever left a dollar bill out for it?"

"No!"

Once she bought in, Nana had a dozen questions about the little dragon. She laughed again when Caro tried to imitate its squeaky voice.

"Aw, baby, I still don't know how this can be, but damn me if that don't sound like a pure delight. Who knew such things could live under the sun."

Nana pitched her voice lower.

"And you know if we both have to spend our time with dragons, at least yours is a cute one."

Caro couldn't make much of a laugh at that one. Mama had shown no sign of leaving Nana's house. At this rate, Caro wouldn't be able to ever go home again.

Caro heard a series of sharp, muffled thunks over the phone, followed by,

"The hell you out there doing, Mama? You're out of cooking sherry."

Caro hadn't heard her mother's voice in three years, but even over a phone line and through a closed door, she could hear the telltale burr that the cooking sherry had gone done Mama's gullet. She wondered whether it was the old bottle that had sat at the back of Nana's cabinet for as long as she could remember.

Was it too much to hope that it had turned to poison?

"Don't you worry, Betsy," Nana bellowed into the phone, making sure Mama would hear every word, "I don't mind a bit doing the altar on Sunday. You just rest that ankle. I'll be there at seven-thirty sharp."

"Gawd," Mama said.

"Got it," Caro said. "I'll call you then. I love you."

"You bet."

Caro sat on the floor by the bathroom door to have her cry. She didn't mean to scare the little dragon, but she didn't want to feel alone.

Her phone rang on Saturday afternoon – Nana must've slipped out to the grocery store.

"You okay?" Caro asked when she answered.

There was a long pause, then.

"Huh."

She registered that it was Mama's voice just as the phone beeped to signal the line being cut off.

Crap.

She called Nana at 7:34 the next morning, and Nana picked up on the first ring.

"Caro."

"Nana, are you all right?"

"Sweetie, I am so sorry. I've been so good about keeping my phone on me, I just let it go for a minute."

"Nana. Are you okay."

Oh, the pause was too long.

"What did she do?"

"I'm fine, baby."

"Nana."

"It was just one cigarette and I got butter right on it, my hand'll be fine."

Caro sat down on the floor.

"Honey, I'm fine. I swear."

"Nana, you have to make her leave."

"Well, baby, I think I did. I spent last night at your aunt Betsy's house, and we're headed back to the house after church with Pere John and Sheriff Huntley to make sure. Sheriff's got a locksmith friend who's coming out to change all the locks and help me fix up my windows. But Caro, baby. Your address was in my phone."

Caro lost all ability to remain vertical and lay on the floor.

"You should get a different phone, baby."

Caro's belly dropped at that tone. It wasn't one she heard very often. Nana tried hard not to let her down. But it happened. Nana wasn't a superhero.

"What else, Nana?"

"Baby, I'm sorry."

"I know you are, Nana. What else?"

"You know I always kept my Christmas tin in the same place."

Always. Caro had stolen from it once or twice – never more than a couple of dollars for candy, until the day Nana caught her and said "don't be like your Mama, Caro. The road's too hard."

She'd never touched it again, and it wasn't because of a hard damn road.

"She'll probably drink it all up, sweetheart."

"Was it enough for bus fare?"

"It was."

There was a long silence. Caro enjoyed how cold and hard the floor was. She was glad she hadn't gotten around to buying a rug. Her shoulder blades ached against the wood, so there was one part of her not filled up with sickness and worry.

"She'll probably drink it all up," Nana repeated.

Probably. But not certainly.

"I'm so sorry, baby," Nana said.

"I know."

Then she remembered her manners.

"It's okay, Nana. You didn't do anything."

"That's half the trouble, isn't it?"

Caro would never agree to that aloud.

"Let's just hope you're right and she goes on a bender in Baton Rouge."

"I love you, sweetheart," Nana said, her voice miserable.

"I love you too. I'll send you my new number."

She turned the phone off. No use in courting trouble.

But she wasn't going to sleep, not with the idea that Mama might show up at the door, expecting food, booze, the bed, to be the center of all attention. To have her every whim obliged on pain of broken bones, property destruction, and plain viciousness.

Caro watched TV (looked at the TV without registering what was on it) for several hours, until her eyes felt coated in sand. She had gone through hungry and out the other side to a queasy exhaustion.

How Mama would laugh at all the change on the floor. Before she picked it all up and pocketed it.

Caro reached for her wallet on the table next to the sofa. She had five quarters in the change pocket. She tossed them onto the floor in front of the sofa and wrapped up in the quilt aunt Betsy made for her high school graduation. May as well make a little happiness in the house.

And boy howdy did she. She dozed a bit, so she had no idea how much time had passed by the time she woke to see the little dragon hopping around the quarters on its little claws. She had always thought the word "scamper" was a dumb word, until she saw it in action by a miniature imaginary creature.

"Rar raaaaar!" it squeaked.

And she couldn't help the choked-off sob she made – it was such a relief to see happiness.

The dragon froze and stared at her. Caro stared back, keeping her hands inside the quilt and her head still, but not bothering to hide her face.

After a long pause, the dragon blinked at her, titled its head back and forth. She blinked back.

It sniffed. Caro sniffed.

The dragon laid one claw experimentally on a quarter, and Caro blinked again.

"Go ahead," she said in a soft voice.

The dragon startled, but it didn't move. It tilted its head again.

"They're for you. Take them."

It waited a long time, moving its claw fractionally, until the moment when it lifted the quarter to its mouth and skittered on three legs down the back hallway. She thought maybe she had scared it for good, given the length of quiet afterward. Long after she'd given up, she saw it creeping along on the floor, hunched down, its triangular head angling toward her as it passed.

The knot in her chest let go. The dragon went totally still when she sniffed in an unsuccessful attempt to stop the tears rolling out of her.

"Sorry," she whispered. "I'm just really glad you came back."

The little dragon huffed at her. Caro wiped her face on the quilt, and by the time she looked up, the dragon was gone with a second quarter.

It didn't hesitate to come back for the third one. By the fifth one, it didn't even pause. It sauntered casually past the sofa and lifted the coin straight to its mouth.

"Rrr!" it squeaked.

"You're welcome," she said, and it was enough to let her sleep.

The knock she dreaded came two days later. She'd had a very uncomfortable conversation with her boss, who shocked Caro to her bones by calling HR on speakerphone and asking them to get started on transferring Caro's desk to the badge-only floor.

"Do you have a picture of her?" he asked. "Get one to security and they'll make sure she doesn't get in the building. You want somebody to travel back and forth with you?"

Caro cried a little bit, much to her horror.

"Look, I don't care how much you try to pull this 'y'all don't bother about lil ole me' crap," Aly said at the gym. "I'm coming over on Saturday, and I'm staying until you find out for sure that you're not getting any unwanted visitors. Pay me in pancakes."

That had made her cry a little again.

So she had a little steel in her spine by the time the door rattled. Was a fifteen-year-old restraining order from Louisiana in force in Chicago? She had no idea.

"Caroline, it's your mama, open up!"

Caro tried to will herself to grasp the doorknob and was unsuccessful.

"Caroline! I saw the light on, I've been traveling a whole day and night, darlin, don't you want to see your mama after all this time?"

She pounded on the door again.

"Open the fucking door, Caroline."

Her neighbors would be able to hear all this. Her neighbors seemed like nice people. They'd try to help, if they thought there was trouble. Trying to get between Mama and what she wanted was a great way to get hurt.

She opened the door. The grimace on Mama's face morphed into something like a smile.

"Caroline."

She pushed past Caro into the living room and looked around, clearly displeased. She was still taller than Caro, still broad-shouldered. But her skin hung loose on her frame, aside from her round belly, and she looked a decade older than her early fifties.

Friends ought to take care of one another, Caro thought.

Mama's best friend, ethanol, didn't take good care of anybody.

"The hell kind of dump is this?" Mama said. "Can't afford anything modern?"

Caro remembered that she was a grown-ass adult and not a terrified elementary schooler.

"You're more than welcome not to stay," she said.

Mama rounded on her with a well-remembered expression: narrow eyes, lower jaw jutted out, cheeks dark with more than the standard burst capillaries.

"What makes you think you can talk to me that way?" she said, grabbing Caro's arm. "I'm your mother, you show some respect."

Caro shrugged hard, trying to pull her arm free, but Mama's grip was as fierce as her snarl.

"Don't you fight me, girl, I know every trick you've got."

"Let me go."

"You don't tell me what to do, Caroline."

"You let me go!"

Caro pulled. Her instant of calm had devolved into the weak-kneed helplessness that dogged her every time she saw her mother. She heard her own breath. She would lose. She always lost. Mama was a juggernaut. Everything fell down in her presence. Everything had always fallen down.

"You straighten up now, girl, I won't have –"

Mama's face went vaguely green, her eyes wide. A calm corner of Caro's mind saw that the sclera were yellow.

"What," Mama croaked, looking over Caro's shoulder.

"Rrrrrrr!"

Caro turned. The little dragon was barely three feet away from them, tiny white teeth bared and its back end wriggling like a cat about to pounce.

"No! No, run!" she yelled, pulling so hard that she wrenched her arm free, although the sleeve of her sweater tore.

The dragon hissed.

"The hell is that," Mama whispered.

"Oh, don't," Caro said, then backpedaled when the dragon jumped.

She landed hard on her butt and stayed planted, mouth open, while the dragon leapt at Mama's knees, banked off them, whirled around on the floor, and jumped again, making its squeaky growl the whole time. Its little claws stuck in Mama's clothing while it climbed her, shrieking in a rasp. Mama stayed frozen and gaping until it reached waist height, then she batted at it and cried out.

The dragon latched onto her hand with its mouth; Mama yelled again and waved her arm. The dragon let go, arched in mid-air, and landed on her shoulder, scrabbling around on her back while Mama pounded her own shoulders, turning in a circle. The dragon kept squeaking "rar rar" and head-butting her between the shoulder blades. Caro could see little spots of blood along Mama's arms and seeping through her shirt. The dragon moved so fast that sometimes it was a blur, crawling up and down Mama's body, pausing only to head-butt her or bite.

"The hell is this?" Mama yelled, "What the hell is going on?"

The dragon hopped onto Mama's shoulder and dug in, then clamped its jaws around her earlobe.

Mama screamed.

Caro felt a vast hysteria rising up from her guts.

Over the sound of Mama's shouts and the dragon's squeaks, Caro heard a firm knock at the door and a muffled voice,

"Neighbor? Everything all right in there?"

Whatever this was, she could answer that question.

"No!" she shouted, "it's not!"

The door slammed inward, and the non-rat-seeing neighbor jumped inside, her dreadlocks flying like Medusa's own snakes. She glanced from Mama, to Caro, back to Mama again.

"What?"

"Get this damn thing off me!" Mama yelled.

The dragon squeaked one more time for good measure, then dropped to the ground. Mama lunged for it; it scrabbled briefly against the wood floor and took off for the hallway. Caro lunged to get between it and Mama –

Who was on her knees, her arms pinned back by the neighbor, eyes wide, her chin shiny with spit.

"What was it?" Mama said in a hoarse voice.

"Are you all right, sweetie?"

There was no sign of that dreamy look in her neighbor's eye: this glance was all business.

"I'm okay. I'm not hurt," Caro said.

And then, "I'm not hurt," with a laugh.

"The hell was it?"

"I think you should leave now," the neighbor said, tugging so that Mama grunted and climbed to her feet with a stumble.

"What was it?"

"I can tell by your voice you're not from here," the neighbor said. "Why don't you get on home, now?"

"She came on the bus," Caro said.

Mama had left a bag in the hallway. There was a return bus ticket in the side pocket. Open ended. Of course.

"Are you stupid?" Mama barked when the artist crowded her into the hallway and pressed the ticket into her hand. "Didn't you see that thing?"

"This is a safe place," the neighbor said, staring up at Mama. "Protected. I don't think you're a very safe person. You should leave now."

"I'm not damn well –"

Must've been some kind of martial arts training. Anyhow, whatever the artist did to Mama's elbow, Mama went down the stairs with her and out the door.

"I'm not leaving my daughter in this hell hole with some kind of goddamn monster," Mama said at the end.

The dramatic intensity of this was greatly lessened by her saying it through a cab window.

"Oh, I think you are," the neighbor said. "I think you're leaving her here for good."

She slapped the cab, and it left.

"Well!" she said, "sorry about your door! I'll make sure Mike knows to put that on my rent and not yours."

"I don't even know how to thank you," Caro said.

"Oh honey," the neighbor said. "Just bake me some brownies or something some time. It all comes out in the wash."

She peered into Caro's apartment on the way back upstairs.

"I didn't know this place was protected quite so *literally*. I'm definitely going to use that."

Caro lay on the floor in front of her sofa and took a while to alternate between hysterical laughter and hysterical sobs. It seemed the thing to do.

When her voice felt as if it might be trustworthy, she called Nana, who took her own turns between laughing and crying during the high points of the story and set Caro off again.

Caro didn't see the dragon the first night, and fretted. The second night, she put down coins and sat on the sofa. The dragon came out a couple of hours after dark, walking slowly.

"Are you okay?" she whispered.

The dragon swiveled its little head toward her and heaved a squeaky sigh.

It looked around at the coins on the floor and sighed again; put a penny in its mouth and walked slowly toward the back hallway, exhaustion plain in every scale on its tiny body.

"Oh!" Caro said, and put her hands to her chest, laughed a little.

She gathered up the coins and took them to the hallway next to the bathroom door.

"Rrr!" the dragon squeaked when it saw her sitting there, the coins in her hands. But it took them from her, one by one, disappearing in between into a shadow under the sink that during daytime was a plain piece of wall. Up close, its body was hot, and it smelled of copper.

"Hff!" it sniffed when it took the last one.

"You're welcome," she said. "Go get some rest."

"Oh baby, I know it's all my fault," Nana said on the phone the next day. "I just couldn't stop her."

"It's okay, Nana. It's all okay."

"How are you going to thank your little friend?"

"I've got a good plan."

She went to the bank and stood in line to see an actual teller. Slid a twenty across the counter.

"I'd like to exchange this, please, for dollar coins. The gold Sacagawea ones, if you have them."

Our Lady of the Wasteland

Carly Racklin

Carly Racklin is a writer, hobbyist illustrator, and bird lover from New Jersey. She possesses a BA in English with a concentration in Creative Writing from Arcadia University. Her work has previously appeared in Mirror Dance, Bird's Thumb, Corvus Review, Quiddity, and more.

It wasn't all that long ago. A few weeks, give or take. Lots of folks have come and gone since then. Maybe you remember it—the dust storm that swept through. It was a wicked one.

I met an angel in that storm. And not just any angel, either. An angel in a red scarf, carrying an axe on her back. You've heard of her, haven't you? You must've. Wouldn't be surprised if even the buzzards started telling the tale.

Anyhow, I was making my way to this here camp. The air was full of rust and ash and not much else. Only way I knew I was on the road was 'cause I felt it under my boots. The storm had sprung up outta nowhere, so fierce my goggles felt about as sturdy as wet paper. Somehow I managed to keep walking. No idea how long for. All I know is that the wind just about knocked me clean off my feet, then there she was. That scarf looked endless, whipping around in every direction at once. Like one of those flags that used to hang outside the havens, if you can remember.

No, she didn't have wings. Where'd you hear that?

No, no wings. No shoes, either. Just one of those old motorcycle helmets with the tinted glass. And a ragged, patchwork dress, made out of a quilt. Stopped me in my tracks, she did. Beat the storm to it.

I've heard most of the rumors, all the stories about how she only shows up on the darkest nights, driest days—the moments folks tend to think'll be their last. Never gave 'em much thought, to be honest with you.

Folks'll make up all sorts of things to put their kids and fears to bed. The longer you last in a place like this, the more you let your fears just tire themselves out. Fear's a heavy thing to carry. Eventually you just run out of room for it.

I've never been much afraid of anything, really. Except dying. But out here, that doesn't count for much. It's like saying you're thirsty. Just the way of things.

When she came out of the dust with that axe on her back, I damn near thought she was Death come to drag me kicking and screaming down to perdition. But she wasn't. She was just the opposite—a miracle. A miracle on two whole, dark legs.

Before the storm showed up, there was no sign of another soul out on that highway. She was barely a step or two in front of me by the time I saw her. Could've taken that helmet right off if I wanted. See the face no one's ever seen. But I didn't. Didn't even think of it then. The helmet just felt like enough of a face already, I guess. Plus, there was no ignoring that axe. Hellish thing, it was—half a sawblade jammed into a baseball bat and wrapped in rusty wire. But ...well, thinking about it now, I don't think she would've used it.

I didn't move a muscle, not at first. The dust started to creep under the rim of my goggles, then she held out one of her hands to me. I just stared. Was still a little caught up thinking she was some kinda monster, or a ghost or something. Can you blame me? I never paid any mind to the stories. A guardian angel? What business did heaven have out here? I always thought that God died with the rest of the world. Burned right up with the trees and laughter and every scrap of goodness in strangers' hearts.

Turns out I was wrong. About a few things.

I took her hand. Bare, like her feet, and impossibly soft. Like it was brand new.

The wind died down a bit, but the air was still too dusty to do anything in but wait. She led me off the road into a little ditch, and we sat together. Sat and just watched each other.

Well, I was watching her. For all I knew, there was nothing but hot air holding up that helmet. I still don't know what she's made of, but it must be good.

Holy, even.

Whatever she is, this world needs her. Somebody's gotta watch over it.

Now, I've heard all the theories folks have. Spouted some of my own, too. Like that she's part of some underground government operation to get the world right-side up again. I don't believe 'em. Some things don't need explaining. They just need doing. I ain't gonna question who or what it is that does 'em.

It's like that old saying—how's it go? Something about a horse's mouth.

Anyway. Where was I, now? Right, the dust storm.

We waited. And waited. Eventually it passed on over, and you could open your mouth without getting dirt in your teeth. She pulled out a canteen and handed it to me. Just like that, like it was the simplest thing in the world. Like wilder folks wouldn't have killed her for it. I was skeptical, of course. You'll die real fast if you don't question some things. I shook the canteen around, smelled it, looked inside. Seemed normal. And damn, was I thirsty. It was like she knew.

The canteen was full of the sweetest, cleanest water I ever tasted in my life. I must've drunk a gallon of it, but that little thing never ran dry. Never felt even a drop less than full. Let me tell you, I thought I really *had* died and made it to heaven. But no, heaven made it here. Better late than never, I guess.

Funny, ain't it? The way things work out?

When I'd had my fill, I handed the canteen back and watched her some more. This time, though, it felt like she was watching me, too.

Then she talked to me.

How'd I know she was an angel? You been listening at all? I'd love to hear your theories. Tell me, kid, what else could she have been? I'll wait.

No, nothing? Well then.

Her voice. It was softer than I expected it to be. Not soft as in frail, just gentle. Young and old all at once. Found it strange at first, familiar. Then I realized how long it'd been since I'd last heard kindness in somebody's voice. Real kindness. The sort that ain't a mask for need. Mercy me, it was something.

First, she asked me what I was travelling for. Where I was headed. I said this here camp. Heard there was solid shelter around, and like any sensible person, I wanted a piece of it.

She laughed at that, an odd little chirp. Though I couldn't tell what was funny about it. She said it was good to know that sensible folks—sensible *people*, she said—still existed. 'Cause she hadn't met many of those in a long time.

I gave her a look for that one. She laughed again, and asked if I'd do her a favor.

I said sure. Wasn't gonna pass this up.

Then she said—and I'll never forget the words, 'cause they were some of the strangest, most beautiful things I ever heard in my life. She goes, "There are so many people in this world who need help. People who need to be reminded that there's something to believe in. That everything isn't pain, and dust, and survival. People like you, Uzi."

I just about jumped outta my skin then. Hadn't heard my own name in ...can't remember how long. She must've noticed, but she didn't stop. Swore I heard a smile in her voice, though.

"There's hope everywhere," she went on. "Most have just forgotten how to see it. They can no longer perceive light, even when it's all around them. Even when it's growing inside them. There's a light burning inside every one of us, do you know that? You do. I can see it in your eyes. I do my best to help kindle these lights. But I only have two hands, you see. That's why I'd like your help."

I didn't have anything smart to say after hearing something like that. Nobody talks like that anymore. It was one of those moments—like the morning the first bombs fell. You could feel it in the air. Everything was different.

So I told her I'd do whatever she needed.

And so she asked me to tell folks about her. To let anyone and everyone know that someone out there was still listening. That someone would be there when they needed it. But most important, she said, was to tell folks that they had to be there, too. They had to listen, too. Because one lonely angel wasn't gonna fix the world. It's way too big a place for one woman to carry on her back.

I had a feeling she already knew my answer, knew it before she ever found me in the dust. But I liked the sound of that anyway. So I said sure, I'd tell anyone I could. Just like all the others that told me. And so here I am. Can't think of a better place to start than this. Hell, for all I know, maybe she heard about the well and filled up her canteen here. Or maybe not. You'd remember her if she did.

Anyway. That's the story.

You don't have to believe me. I sure didn't, until I met her face to face. Maybe it'll take that much for you, too.

But look around. You're not stupid. There's not all that much left to lose here, but a hell of a lot to save. Like I said before, somebody's gotta watch over this place. Turns out it's not a one-person job. So what do you say?

The world didn't end happy. We can't change that. But maybe, just maybe, we can try and give it a decent epilogue.

Frost

C.L. Spillard

C. L. Spillard was born just in time
to endure the U.K.'s coldest winter of
last century. Until recently a physicist
by profession, she now writes science
fiction, fantasy and satire, sometimes
all at once. She lives in York with her
Russian husband, two almost-bilingual
children, one allotment and nine
solar panels.

So: she came.

Hu Tao, the dissident's daughter.

In reality she didn't have much choice. If the city's Magnate sends you an invitation to his New Year party, you need a good reason to refuse it. Though I suppose mourning may suffice.

I mix her drink. I measure the powder carefully: she is slight.

Her hands tremble as she takes the glass. I smile. The shy ones are the best.

The glass slips and shatters on the marble floor. I curse inwardly, but etiquette demands I hand her mine.

Ah-Mei cleans up, then discreetly withdraws. Simple servant-girls: what treasures!

"I'm so sorry!" Hu Tao blushes. "Please, let me get you another."

I watch her go to the buffet and mix bitters. She stands erect in straight silk - high-collared, floor-length: a classic. She brings the glass - bows as she hands it me. I notice she has removed her long jewelled hair-pin. One frost-white hair gleams among the otherwise perfect raven black. I believe that is my doing.

She raises her drink to mine:

"Drain the glass dry!"

I taste exquisite bitters: the rim of the glass frosted with a circle of salt.

She smiles. "A true Revolutionary can endure bitterness." It is her challenge. I run my finger slowly round the rim and lick the salt with pleasure.

She hides her disgust well.

***

It is late. She has declined my offer and departed: in mourning. A good line, but it will not last forever. The wait will make the conquest all the sweeter.

My neck - my face - grate tired and stiff as I climb into bed.

I am woken by pain shooting across my shoulders. My back aches; I shudder. My teeth grit. This is not good.

I ring for Ah-Mei.

"Fetch the doctor."

She stays put.

"Half the city's in lock-down. Explosion at the Laboratory: a spark, from the New Year fireworks. Doctors are treating hundreds who inhaled the fumes."

Her voice is frost.

"I know who cut safety costs on his newly-acquired asset: my son's workplace."

The shock sets the convulsions off anew. I am racked with pain.

"Hu Tao wishes you peaceful 'Year of the Dog.' She asked me to prepare your suicide note. I have practiced your signature and borrowed your seal. You will die with your reputation in mud, where it belongs."

***

She bows before her father's portrait. She places the letter in the metal stand between the two smoking joss-sticks and lights the paper.

"Dear father,

You have been vindicated: your concerns for the Laboratory's safety justified.

Thank you for teaching me the preparation of Strychnine crystals. I have put the knowledge to good use: he is gone.

Now at last we can bring you home. Home, from the bitter Northern mines where they sent you for speaking out: voicing your fears. Where they told me they couldn't even bury you, in that earth gripped year-round in frost."

She turns: bows to the tiny, white-haired figure beside her.

Her mother smiles as Hu Tao hands back the glittering, hollow hairpin.

Morph

Sarah Pfleiderer

Sarah Pfleiderer is a recent graduate of the University of Evansville with a BFA in creative writing and a minor in gender and women's studies. Her previous publication includes a poem in the Mangrove journal out of The University of Miami.

Dr. Audra Grissom stretched as she woke from her hyper-sleep, groaning as each vertebra popped and clicked back into alignment. She flinched as she placed a bare foot on the floor outside her sleeping pod.

"They couldn't have turned the heat on a little early?" she muttered as she levered herself to standing. Audra made her way to a window as the other scientists crawled out of their pods. Outside, hanging in the dark vacuum of space, was the Inter-Galactic Neutral Space Station. It shone like a mirror shard, its countless solar panels and bright windows beckoning as if it were a celestial lighthouse.

"That's not a bad sight to wake up to, is it?" Audra murmured, her breath ghosting on the reinforced glass.

"Ready, Dr. Grissom?"

The chipper voice of a morning person sounded over her shoulder. She turned and saw one of the chief anthropologists behind her.

"As we could ever hope to be."

***

The scientists and crew of the Abeona met by the cargo bay once their grogginess had abated. The briefing was purely a formality; everyone knew why they were there. Guidelines were recited, packets outlining information they had all memorized years earlier were distributed, and warnings were issued.

"We've maintained a dialogue with the Phytomorphs for three decades now; I don't want anything to jeopardize our relationship, is that clear? We're making history, folks. Let's make sure we're on the right side of it." Audra looked around the room, giving everyone a chance to meet her unflinching gaze. The steeliness of her eyes matched the silver hair she kept cropped around her shoulders. She had started graying in her 30s, but had given up trying to dye it back to its original brown once she hit her 40s. She had no husband or children to keep up appearances for anyway. Besides, the unruly interns back home respected her authority when they thought she was their grandmother's age.

Audra cleared her throat.

"Now for some basics, which I'm sure you are already familiar with, but in case anyone has been living under a rock for the last thirty years—" a quiet chuckle rose from the group.

"The Phytomorphs are the first and only alien species humans have come into contact with in all of recorded history. They are generally shorter in stature, get their energy through a type of photosynthesis, and have cultures as varied as our own. We'll be living and interacting with them for the next few years, so we'll have plenty of time to get to know each other."

Another dry chuckle.

"Does anyone have any questions?"

An impatient silence followed.

"Good. Let's get ready to dock."

The Abeona slid into the docking space, delicate as surgery. The IGNSS was designed with three major wings: one for human habitation, one for the Phytomorphs, and a common central area where the two species would interact and collect data. It was a horseshoe, and Audra liked to think that it was tilting upward.

Objects were unloaded from the Abeona's cargo hold: clothing from all over the world, both modern and historical, tools and weapons, examples of food that was to be offered to the Phytomorphs, books, textiles, samples of artwork and music, records of monumental historic events, photographs of animals and architecture. Every physical representation of Earth's cultures and its cumulative history. The Phytomorphs would be arriving with their own collection.

The schedules were remarkably synced, with the humans arriving only days before the Phytomorphs. They met in one of the many conference rooms on the station. Audra and the other scientists tried to present themselves with professional decorum and stifle their gasps as the first Phytomorphs filed into the room. Audra wiped her clammy palms on her thighs, and her ears throbbed with her heartbeat. She had to bite her lower lip to keep from grinning like an expectant mother. After decades of work and billions of dollars in funding, it was all going to be worth it.

Their skin was leathery and heavily ridged, and had growths clustering along their joints that resembled lichen or moss. The lower halves of their bodies, if one were to assign an Earth-like equivalent, were vaguely tree-trunk in shape, with sprawling sentient roots. Their faces were mostly featureless, but had two massive green eyes in the same bright verdancy as tree leaves backlit by a summer sun. They moved like an octopus, each limb moving independently so that the Phytomorphs appeared to undulate across the floor. The Phytomorph leading the group reached out its hands in welcome, palms upward. Audra placed her hands lightly on top of the alien's. Its mouth opened, and the communicator around its neck translated the thrumming gargle:

"Welcome, friends. We yearn to begin this journey of peace and learning."

Audra spoke her own gratitude and welcome; a similar communicator hung around her neck. The Phytomorphs buzzed as they extended their personal welcomes to the other scientists. Audra remained with the one who had greeted her.

Over the past decades, this was the one Phytomorph she had been in contact with the most. Audra had clocked in a staggering amount of overtime at the Galactic Communications Lab, receiving and imparting messages to the aliens. From the first static-filled thrums caught by satellites to the fully-furnished blueprints for the IGNSS, Audra had maintained constant contact. Over the years, they had formed a close bond, and she had secretly nicknamed him "Ziggy" after her favorite 1970s musician. The androgynous spider-limbed alien fit the bill quite nicely.

"It is wonderful to finally meet you," Audra said, smiling. Ziggy's root-like limbs fluttered happily against the floor.

"It is equally pleasant to meet you, friend Doctor Audra." Ziggy was her alien equivalent, with as strong a passion and curiosity for humans as she had for the Phytomorphs. She gripped his rough hands once more, and felt the ridges press into her skin.

During the course of the next three months, human scientists and Phytomorphs met and collated their data. The mission was purely academic, but friendships inevitably formed. There was awkwardness at times, and the leading anthropologists on board helped the humans through the worst of the culture shock. The other discomfort lay in the acknowledgement of the negative sides of humanity. The fact of human cruelty was delicately addressed. There was no way around it. During one meeting, Ziggy asked,

"Why do you care so deeply for some humans, but harm so many others?"

Audra paused before responding.

"We are proud and fearful creatures, and sometimes we let those feelings get in the way of everything else."

"You are a deeply flawed species." Ziggy responded, tilting his head to one side. Audra gave a quiet, wry smile.

"Yes, we are. But we wouldn't be us without them."

"We ourselves are not perfect, but we have never committed such..." Ziggy gestured to both the holograph projector and information packets on the table. The Holocaust. Cambodian genocide. Armenian genocide. American slavery. The bombing of Hiroshima. The Trail of Tears. He picked up an information packet, and flipped through the color images of riots and mass graves. A twiggy finger rested on the image of a screaming mother holding her child. There was a heavy silence in the room. Audra finally broke it with a small sigh.

"We can be done for the day, if you wish."

Ziggy nodded, still staring at the image. Audra picked up her things and left the room, pausing to look back at his hunched figure as he stared blankly at the papers in his hands.

The most popular form of recreation aboard the IGNSS was the solarium at the heart of the station. Massive windows framed the room to let in the light that reflected off the solar panels. This was where both the Phytomorphs came to sun themselves and photosynthesize, and where the humans ate their rehydrated meal packs. It was also fitted with games, books, and lounge areas. It was the largest room on the station, and most of the inhabitants spent their free time there.

One day, Ziggy approached Audra in the solarium after sunning himself by the windows. The root-like tendrils were skittering happily on the linoleum as he rushed to her. His large green eyes shone brightly, and the outline of his body had a pale-yellow glow.

"Friend Doctor Audra! We are performing The Hum tonight. Would you like to join us?"

Audra's breath caught. The Hum was a ceremonial and spiritual gathering that no human had ever witnessed. The Phytomorphs had mentioned it in their discussions with the human scientists, but few details were given. She nodded, and looked over at a few of the Phytomorphs happily chatting by the windows as they fed off the solar rays. They caught her gaze and smiled at her. Audra's stomach twisted in anticipation.

***

Audra met them in one of the gathering rooms on the Phytomorph side of the station later that night. The lights were dim when she entered, and it took her a few seconds to adjust. The Phytomorphs were sitting in a circle, softly conversing in their native languages. They all must have been sunning themselves recently, for their lichens were thick and plush, and a soft haze clung to their bodies. Ziggy found her and gestured to the empty space next to him. Once she sat down, he nudged her shoes and wiggled his own tuber-like extremities. Audra took off the offending shoes and socks and set them behind her. She was mildly embarrassed by the smell of her feet in the crowded room, but the Phytomorphs didn't seem to notice.

Slowly, they began to hum. There was a rustling sound, and Audra saw them intertwining their roots with the alien next to them. She felt the roots thread between her toes and coil up her calves. Her hands and forearms were also ensnared, and soon all the Phytomorphs were entangled with the others in an inter-connected ring. Audra was immediately reminded of some fact from a high school biology course about mycelia and earthen root systems.

The thrumming grew louder, and the aliens started swaying, like grasses caught in an afternoon breeze. The hair on the backs of Audra's arms stood on end, and she was filled with an envel-oping sense of contentment. The hum grew louder still, until the entire room seemed to vibrate. She looked around her. The Phytomorphs had closed their eyes. She closed her own and was hit with a wave of sensation. Every heartbeat of the Phytomorphs around her echoed in her own chest. It was as though she was inhabiting all of them at once, while they were inhabiting her. Tears began to streak down Audra's cheeks, but she couldn't have been able to explain why. She moved in harmony with them, rev-eling in the feeling of oneness. All thoughts emptied out of her mind, and she was no longer aware of time passing. Everything was consumed by the swaying, purring, wholeness of The Hum.

When it finally ended and the Phytomorphs' roots untangled from their neighbor's, Audra was surprised that she felt disap-pointed. The close intimacy brought on by The Hum was fading, and she was lonely in her own body. The Phytomorphs were slow in dispersing, as if they too didn't want the sensation to end. She placed a hand on Ziggy's shoulder and felt the familiar hard ridges of his skin under her palm.

"Thank you."

He smiled, the thin slit of his mouth broadening.

"Do humans have a Hum?"

Audra shook her head.

"Nothing even close."

Ziggy nodded solemnly.

"That would explain why you are cruel, sometimes." There was no malice or mockery in his voice, he was simply stating fact. He drifted off to join the other Phytomorphs as they went back to their own dwelling spaces. Audra took her time walking back to the human side of the station, slowly piecing herself back together.

In the common room, men and women were scattered, absorbed in their various hobbies. A woman knitted in the corner, listening to an old recorded podcast. Someone was hunched over a sketchbook. The only sound was the soft burr of the station and the whisper of pages and yarn. Audra recognized the chief anthropologist who had spoken to her on the Abeona. She called his name and waved. He gave a distracted nod, too immersed in the book propped on his knee. Audra went to bed feeling hollow.

***

Audra wasn't the only human Ziggy interacted with. He followed the other scientists and showered them with questions.

He cooed and exclaimed over the slightest thing, whether it be someone tying their shoe or cracking their knuckles. He was endlessly curious and adored the humans to such an extent that even Audra was amused.

One afternoon, six months after they arrived at the station, Ziggy joined Audra at her usual spot in the solarium.

"Friend Doctor Audra!"

It was quiet in the solarium that day, and his excited voice felt jarring against the haze of sun, and the Phytomorphs standing in a silent forest by the windows. He sat down across from her, his roots coiling around the chair legs. Audra glanced from his animated face to the Phytomorphs at the windows. Instead of their usual gargling chatter, they were hushed, focused on absorbing every ray that hit their skin.

"Are they doing all right?" Audra nodded towards the windows, "they seem...different today."

Ziggy glanced back at them and shrugged, "I know they've been really hungry lately."

"Hungry?" Audra shifted in her seat, "we can change the schedules, so you have more time to sun yourselves."

She withdrew a pen, and began making a note on the back of her hand, but Ziggy stopped her.

"No, no, do not worry yourself. I'm sure it's nothing." He gave a reassuring smile, but the sight of the Phytomorphs silently clustered by the windows nagged at her for the rest of her meal.

***

Later that day, Audra visited the data files on the human side of the station. They were kept in a separate room, as if the super-computer got flustered and couldn't think properly if it had to share living space. Audra scanned her ID and logged in, the soft whirring and beeps of the fiber optics and motherboards around her doing little to calm her nerves. She pulled up information about the Phytomorphs' dietary habits. Throughout the course of the study, the human and aliens were simultaneously observing each other. Audra had to admit, it had taken some time to get used to entering in the amount of time she'd slept, how much food she consumed at meals, the weekly weight updates, and records of how she used her free time. But in return, she had access to this. She found the dietary summary for all twenty-five Phytomorphs on board. She bit her lip as she looked over the numbers. The amount of time they collectively spent sunbathing in the solarium had increased, but the end-of-day evaluations reported the majority of the Phytomorphs feeling weak and tired.

"What is happening to you guys?" she murmured under her breath as she double-checked the numbers. It wasn't a mistake. The Phytomorphs were struggling to photosynthesize. They were starving.

Audra called an emergency meeting with the other human scientists. They gathered in a conference room, whispering to each other in confusion. Audra relayed what she'd found.

"It can't be the solar ray apparatus, we built it from their instructions. Something is happening to them. I don't know if it's a type of infection or virus or what, but I get the sense that it has to do with us." She pursed her lips. "I'll be the first to admit, we've gotten too close."

A biologist in the back of the room piped up, "So, what are you suggesting?"

"I'll be honest with you. I'm not entirely sure, yet. So much has gone into this mission, but I'm concerned that it's been compromised."

Someone else spoke, "If we're influencing their biology this much, I suggest we abort."

Audra felt a spike of adrenaline.

"What? It took us sixteen years to get here, not to mention the decades of work since we first—"

The person speaking stepped forward. It was Dr. Muir, one of the philosophers on board. His focus was ethics and epistemology.

"Dr. Grissom, we know you have a lot invested in this mission, more than anyone. But when we set out to make contact with these creatures, our number one priority was to strictly observe and collect information, not to influence their behaviors. From what you've told us, it would appear that our principle command has been violated. Would you not agree?"

Audra paused, considering her words.

"I hear you, and I understand the need for caution. However, I do think the decision to abort the mission is a bit premature. I suggest we continue to monitor this closely, and if the situation gets worse, we reconvene and discuss our options from there. That seems reasonable, yes?" Audra passed her gaze across the room, daring anyone to argue with her.

***

A few weeks later, the situation hadn't improved. The humans had altered the schedule so the Phytomorphs had more hours to be in the solarium, and the solar panels were double- and triple-checked by the engineers on board, but the aliens continued to grow weaker.

Audra had just sat down for lunch when Ziggy joined her at her usual spot in the solarium.

"What is the material which you are ingesting?" he asked. The other Phytomorphs were standing by the windows, faces uplifted to the light reflecting from the solar panels.

"Rehydrated steak and broccoli. Basically a TV dinner." Audra smiled at her own joke.

"May I try some?"

Audra froze. This was new.

"Um. Are you sure? I don't think—" She thought he would reach for the broccoli. Instead he extended a hand and selected a pre-cut cube of steak. Before Audra could object, Ziggy popped it into his mouth. He chewed slowly. Audra's mouth hung open as he swallowed. This was the first recorded case of a Phytomorph ingesting physical food. The sight of such a botanical creature gnawing on a dead animal felt inherently wrong. Ziggy's twiggy fingers drummed on the table, considering.

"That was most interesting."

Audra pulled the tray closer to her.

"What type of sustenance did you say that was?"

She put her napkin over the uneaten food. Her appetite was gone.

"That was steak. From a cow."

Ziggy nodded thoughtfully. From across the room, a few Phytomorphs were curiously eying the pair. Audra's face flushed, feeling strangely guilty like she'd been caught giving alcohol to a minor. She stood with her half-eaten plate.

"I'm sorry, I just remembered that I have a meeting I need to get to."

Ziggy nodded, and she left. The white lie gnawed at her as she walked down the hallway, and she couldn't shake the image of Ziggy's mouth closing around that cube of steak.

***

The room buzzed as Audra told the other scientists what had happened. One of the biologists spoke up.

"I didn't think they even had a digestive system."

The room grew louder as other people voiced their own questions:

"Evolution can't work this quickly."

"Is this happening to all of them, or just a few?"

"Is it some sort of virus? Could we catch it?"

"So, an alien had some steak. Is it really that big a deal?"

Dr. Muir raised a hand, and the room hushed. He enunciated each word carefully.

"This is even more reason to withdraw. If we are endangering these beings, intentional or not, then we need to cease all interaction. And I think it's obvious that our presence is affecting them. I don't think any one of us wants to be responsible for these creatures' suffering."

A weighty silence filled the room. No one could think of a worthy response. Audra cleared her throat to rid herself the lump that was forming there.

"All right then. We return to Earth."

***

Audra's chest felt heavy as she sat down at her next meeting with Ziggy. It would take the humans a few days to get everything sorted, and Audra wanted to see her friend again before she left. He immediately noticed the change in her demeanor, and reached out to grip her hands folded on the table in front of her.

"Friend Doctor Audra, what is making you so upset?"

She gave his hands a friendly squeeze.

"We're leaving. I know it hasn't been the allotted time we agreed on at the beginning of this project. But we feel that it has been... corrupted."

His green eyes crinkled and he withdrew his hands.

"Corrupted? How do you mean?"

Audra paused, then gave him a sideways look.

"Have you felt any different lately? Noticed any changes?"

He shrugged.

"Nope, not that I can tell. I know some of the other aliens haven't been feeling well lately though."

Audra opened her mouth to ask something else, but it clicked shut. The other aliens. She sat back in her chair.

"What do you mean 'other aliens?'"

"The green ones. The ones that hang out by the windows all the time and have tree roots for feet. We try to keep our distance in case it's contagious"

"You called them aliens. You called the Phytomorphs aliens. Why would you do that?"

He quirked his head at her.

"That's what they are, aren't they?"

***

All the humans were packing to leave, importing any remaining data to the Abeona's servers and finalizing any loose ends. It had taken them a few weeks to reroute the Abeona's flight plans and make the necessary changes to the hyper-sleep pods. All the Earth artifacts were brought back on board, and the living quarters on the IGNSS were emptied. The Phytomorphs, if they were confused, were too distracted to show it. Most of them spent their time in the solarium, bathing in the sunlight at all hours. The others drifted through the hallways and followed the humans, asking to help and for details of their departure.

A few hours before the Abeona was scheduled to detach from the IGNSS, all the human scientists were packed and had boarded the Abeona, tidying away any last items before their sixteen-year sleep. Audra wandered the empty station. Her chest ached at the prospect of leaving, and she trailed her fingertips along the walls. She had spent most of a lifetime preparing for this mission, and had a hand in almost every aspect, from the layout of the conference rooms to the collection of human artifacts. It felt like saying goodbye to a child.

There were no Phytomorphs undulating through the hallways on their curious limbs. She checked their wing of the IGNSS.

Their homey, rounded dwellings were empty. She made her way to the center of the horseshoe.

Audra's breath caught in the back of her throat as she walked in on the Phytomorphs in the solarium. Some were clustered around the food dispensing unit, tearing open the remaining meal packs. Others were weakly pressing themselves against the windows, as if hoping they could pass through the transparent film and become one with the rays of light. Small dried clumps littered the floor at their feet, and Audra gagged. The lichens and mosses that had once bloomed so thick and rich across their shoulders were shriveling and falling off. Their eyes were dull, their limbs atrophied. She scanned the room for Ziggy. There, at the center of the frenzied cluster. She pushed her way past the oblivious Phytomorphs, who ignored both her and their starving companions at the windows.

"Dr. Audra!" Ziggy cried when she finally broke into the center of the cluster. Scattered about his feet were empty packages of food, and crumbs had settled onto his skin like mushroom spores. Gripped in each hand was a chunk of dripping meat. He grinned at her. Audra didn't realize Phytomorphs had teeth.

"What are you doing?" She panted. Ziggy shrugged and glanced around the circle.

"Just having some lunch." He opened his mouth to take a bite, and the sight of those new pearlescent shards poised above the dripping hunk in his fist filled Audra with a horror she'd never known. Lunging, she reached toward the meat in his hand. Ziggy calmly moved out of reach and regarded her with mild confusion.

"Dr. Audra, there's plenty, you don't have to take mine."

"You're not supposed to be eating that! You don't even have a stomach!"

Ziggy put a hand on his hip and cocked it to the side in a gesture that would have been comical under different circumstances.

"I don't see why you guys have to hog all the good stuff." He took a bite, juices running down his chin and forearm.

Audra gestured to the Phytomorphs wasting away by the windows. Most were crumpled on the ground now, too weak to move.

"Look at your people! What's happening to them?"

Ziggy peered over her shoulder at the other aliens. His eyes were smaller and had lost their otherworldly vibrancy. A disgusted sneer twisted the corners of his mouth.

"Hell if I know. Between you and me, those things always freaked me out."

Audra's mind spun. She recalled the intimacy of The Hum and was overwhelmed with loss.

She gripped Ziggy's shoulders, but cried out as soon as her skin came into contact. It was soft and yielding, almost...fleshy. The hard ridges that had adorned his skin when they first met were gone. She snatched her hands back and a great swath of lichen came with, crumbling into smaller pieces as it was removed. Ziggy didn't appear to notice.

"What's gotten into you, Audra? Is everything all right?"

She shook her head and looked down at her hands. Specks of dried lichen clung to her palms.

"I think I'm going to be sick," she murmured, eyes scanning the room for a trashcan. Ziggy took a step toward her. A step. A pronounced, single movement. Not the fluid crawling of roots and tendrils. Audra looked down and saw that Ziggy's mass of roots had condensed into two stocky trunks. Legs. The nausea hit her with full force and she vomited on the ground. Ziggy leapt out of the way. The image of those makeshift legs and their jerky, unsure movements like those of a newborn deer made her stomach heave again. She staggered backward and bumped into the other feasting Phytomorphs. Stumbling, she fell to the ground. Suddenly she was surrounded by countless pairs of those crude legs. Crumbling bits of lichen drifted down as the Phytomorphs brushed against each other in their wild grasping for food, heedless of their companions or the human cowering on the floor at their feet. As Audra lay panting, an intrusive thought broke through the adrenaline: *Were we ever this ravenous?* She scrambled to her feet and rushed out of the solarium. She could hear Ziggy shouting after her.

"Audra! Wait!"

Ziggy broke free from the horde of aliens and chased after her. She looked behind and saw him running, stumbling every few feet as his legs adjusted to their new movements. His arms were splayed out for balance and his voice was desperate as he called out her name. Audra's heart lodged itself behind her larynx as she saw his movements become more sure, more confident. Soon he was running with natural ease, long legs stretching out almost gracefully.

They passed through the human wing of the station before Audra stopped. Ziggy approached sheepishly. She turned to face him. She was caught between his pleading gaze and the airlock doors behind her that would lead to the Abeona's hyper-sleep pods.

"We're about to leave, what do you want?"

"Take me with you." Ziggy panted as he caught his breath. Deep furrows formed in Audra's brow at his request.

"What?"

"I don't want to be left alone with these aliens. I want to come with you." She could see the remains of his meal sticking to the corners of his mouth.

Audra shook her head. Anger was starting to boil in the space where nausea had been. She gestured to the solarium back down the hallway.

"Those are your people! Those are your people and they're dying! Don't you remember The Hum?"

Ziggy didn't respond but stepped forward to take her hand in his. She looked down at it. Fingernails, hard and pink as shells, grew from pale crescents. She pressed her own thumb against his whorled fingerprints. She took her hand away and moved back from him. In the solarium, with the other Phytomorphs crowded around and the shock of her nausea, she hadn't been able to get a good look at him. The hardened ridges that had crested his body when they first met seven months ago had softened into...just skin. It became clear to the humans early on that Phytomorphs did not have discernable genders, and that they procreated in a different manner than humans. But Ziggy's new, naked body was unmistakably male. There was no lichen, no tendrils, no roots. Only sturdy muscular limbs.

Goosebumps prickled along Audra's flesh. Flesh that was so similar to his. She shivered and scrubbed at the tiny bumps. Ziggy chuckled lightly.

"See? Not so different, you and I."

Audra's head swam. She knew he was referring to their fleshy skin, but that statement rattled something loose in Audra's mind. *Not so different.* She felt as though her brain was rewinding like one of those ancient VHS tapes:

"You are a deeply flawed species."

"That is why you are cruel, sometimes."

"Is it some sort of virus? Could we catch it?"

A cold sweat clung to her palms, and to the dewy hairs at the back of her neck. Her own human body suddenly felt alien, unknown. *He forgot. What if...we also forgot?*

Ziggy smiled, showing teeth.

"Come, Audra. Let's go home."

Thank You To
Our Supporters

Many thanks to our patrons and supporters, especially:

Anna O'Brien • Cathrin Hagey

Natalie Weizenbaum • S Naomi Scott

Emily Anderson • Fen • J'nae Spano

Martin Cohen • Salomao Becker

Shelly Jones • Tessa N • Tory Hoke

S. Kay Nash • Carly Racklin • GriffinFire

Isabel Cañas • Jen G • Kayla

Liz Warner • Maria Haskins

Suzanne Thackston

Want to see your name here? Become a patron!
patreon.com/lunastation

 patreon

About the Cover Artist

Lâle is a freelance illustrator currently based in Berlin. She specializes in character design, book cover and board games illustration.

You can find more of her work at:

laleann.daportfolio.com

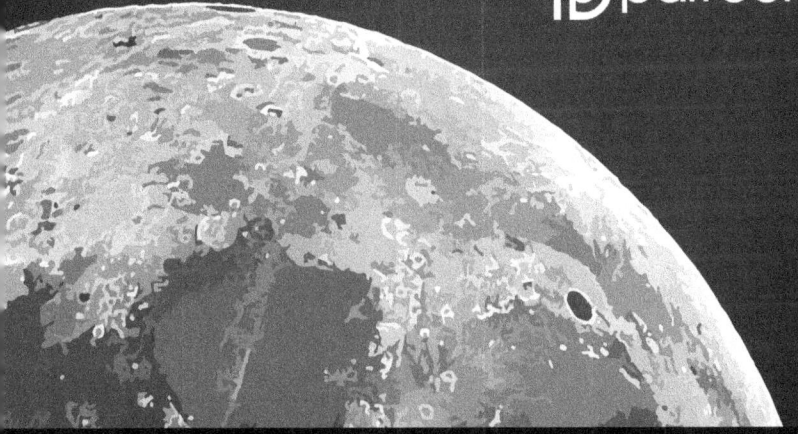